NANCY WARREN

HIGHWAY TO HELLEBORE

VILLAGE FLOWER SHOP
COZY MYSTERY - BOOK 3

Highway to Hellebore, Village Flower Shop Book 3, Copyright © 2023 by Nancy Warren

Cover Design by Lou Harper of Cover Affairs

ISBN: ebook 978-1-990210-61-7

ISBN: print 978-1-990210-60-0

Ambleside Publishing

INTRODUCTION

Beware of men in fast cars...

When a fancy sports car whizzes down the high street of Willow Waters in the Cotswolds, florist and witch Peony Bellefleur senses that it could bring trouble. She is right. Bad boy Dennis Ratslaff left Willow Waters many years ago, and the community breathed a sigh of relief. After a couple of decades in Australia, he's returned with an Aussie accent, a lot of money, and a plan to stay. He's bought a beautiful historic property with an award-winning English country garden that he plans to dig up for his swimming pool.

The neighbors are angry, and the historical society is horrified, but Dennis doesn't care. He's rich, he's romancing the town's most eligible widow, and he'll worry about the rules after he's broken them. But when his digger unearths a major archaeological find, Dennis is forced to stop. Then it turns out there's more than a Roman burial site in his garden...

Meanwhile, the town's most eligible bachelor, and secret

werewolf, has asked Peony out on a date and her mother and housemates all want to help her prepare for the first real date she's had in years.

If you haven't met Rafe Crosyer yet, he's the gorgeous, sexy vampire in *The Vampire Knitting Club* series. You can get his origin story free when you join Nancy's no-spam newsletter at NancyWarrenAuthor.com.

Come join Nancy in her private Facebook group where we talk about books, knitting, pets and life. www.facebook.com/groups/NancyWarrenKnitwits

HIGHWAY TO HELLEBORE

CHAPTER 1

*T*hings don't move quickly in a village like Willow Waters, in the Cotswolds, one of England's prettiest areas. To give you just one example out of countless options, when we voted to change the hanging baskets on the high street from the traditional geraniums and blue lobelia to plants more local to the UK, the discussions of what to replace them with were so long and heated that we missed an entire summer.

Yup, that's right. Not a single hanging basket graced our much-photographed and heavily praised high street.

Our indecision (and lack of urgency) dented our pride at being the most gorgeous village in the vicinity and I, for one, made sure not to let the slow pace around here get the better of me again.

But one thing was guaranteed to shatter our peace. A speeding car. So, when a fancy sports model roared by one June morning at top speed, it was a shock.

I had driven myself and Charity Abbot—who goes by Char, *thank-you-very-much*—and her parrot familiar,

Norman, to the high street of Willow Waters where my flower shop is located. Char worked at Café Roberto, just down the road from Bewitching Blooms, which is my pride and joy. Well, that's not completely true. Really, my farmhouse is my pride and joy, or it will be when I get it completely renovated.

But the shop is where I create and sell gorgeous bouquets of flowers—adding a little witchy magic to the blooms to help the recipients, whether they be celebrating a birthday or mourning someone who's passed. We witches are never allowed to use our magic for personal gain. That's a real no-no, but I believe that adding some extra care—for people who need it—falls into the benevolence category.

I know what you're thinking, but the success of Bewitching Blooms isn't due to magic. Believe me, running a successful business in these times takes more than even my best goodwill spells. We do a great job because we work hard and we care about what we do.

The 'we' here includes my brilliantly (and classically) trained florist, Imogen Billings, who I value as my assistant. My business MBA means I'm better at the general running of the shop and throwing together those bouquets that literally look like they were just thrown together. Still, that casual look does take some talent and time to get right.

Anyway, back to the morning in question. Char and I got out of my beaten-up Range Rover, which also doubles as my delivery van, when the low hum of an intensely powerful sports-car engine could be heard. In less time than it took me to register the rumbling sound, a bright-red flash sped past, practically breaking the sound barrier.

As I said, "Wow, that's a—" Char piped up with, "Lamborghini Aventador Coupe. A real beauty."

I'd been going to say sports car.

Char was extremely conversant with cars. She could identify the year and model from far away. And fix them, too, if need be. She'd been working on the old Citroën truck my husband, Jeremy, had bought just before he died. It had pretty much been a garden ornament, or garden shed ornament really, until she took it apart piece by piece and put it together again. Now it ran perfectly well, and we considered it her vehicle. Char, who was barely in her twenties, named it Frodo.

Parking spots in the village were highly prized, so it was easier for Char to ride in with me and then walk the remaining distance to her job as a barista.

We were both still staring into the distance where the Lamborghini had swiftly disappeared when she said, "I know there's a lot of rich people around here, but a model like that would likely set you back a cool two hundred and eighty grand."

I sucked in my breath. Nearly three hundred thousand pounds? For a car?

There were a lot of wealthy people who had first or second homes in our pretty little village in the Cotswolds. Plenty of them commuted a couple of times a week into London for their fancy jobs in finance, media, or tech—but the Italian Riviera, this was not. With the odd exception, people tended to play down their wealth here, as any show of ostentation was frowned upon in a very British way.

So, this vehicle was certainly new in town. My instinct was to hope that it would keep going. And at the rate they were driving, they'd be in Edinburgh by lunchtime.

In her usual blunt manner, Char said, "Well, I'll be off,

then," and headed toward the coffee shop to open for the morning. Although Char had only been in town a couple of months, she'd already impressed the owner, Roberto, enough to promote her and trust her with the keys. Since I'd taken her in after spotting that she was a fellow witch, I felt proud of her swift success in the village.

Norman called after her, in his Brooklyn accent, which always cracks me up when I hear it from a parrot. "Don't do anything I wouldn't do, Cookie."

She turned and glared at him. "You mean like poop all over the patio tables? Oh, don't worry, I won't. I was the one who had to clean that up, you know."

If a parrot could pout, Norman was an expert. "I got bored," he whined. "It was target practice."

Norman could pout all he liked, but Char had given him a temporary time-out from following her to the coffee shop, since his natural instinct seemed to be to wreak havoc. Never mind that his actual job as a witch's familiar was to protect and aid his witch. Right now, he was stuck with me, in short-flying distance of Char. Or, more accurately, I was stuck with him.

Still, I had laid down the law. If he wanted to parrot-poop target practice, he had to find somewhere else to do it. I thought he'd learned his lesson and maybe even missed Char, because he was being very good when he stayed in the flower shop with me.

A lot of my customers already knew him, as he'd previously been living with Dolores Prescott in the cottage across the street. Poor Dolores had come to an unhappy end, and I think the villagers felt sorry for Norman, probably not realizing that he hadn't been living with Dolores when she passed away. By that point, he'd already discovered that Char was his witch and he was her familiar. In her typical rebellious fashion, Char had fought against him for a while, but it was hopeless. They were a match, and we all knew it.

Norm and I entered Bewitching Blooms. Imogen was closing up for me this evening and wouldn't start for another hour. It was a warm day in June, and I immediately set about watering the flowers in my window boxes and the hanging baskets outside the shop. They got extra thirsty at this time of year, and since the windows were supposed to show off my wares to potential customers, I had to nurture them with extra care.

Not ten minutes went by before I heard that same low buzz of an expensive car engine, which I could already identify as the same Lamborghini that had passed earlier. To my surprise—and horror, if I'm being truthful—it screeched to a halt in front of my shop and then did a sharp turn, pulling in neatly beside my Range Rover in the one and only customer parking spot belonging to my shop.

I felt flustered. I had to be vigilant about who used that spot because, as I explained earlier, parking in Willow Waters, as in most Cotswold villages, was notoriously hard to come by. Oh, the tight-lipped showdowns I'd witnessed over the years about who had the right to park where, and when, and for how long. The Lamborghini driver wouldn't be the first person who thought they could get away with parking in my visitor's spot while slipping off for some sightseeing or shopping.

But that was not going to happen today.

I was getting ready to tell Speedy Gonzalez to move on

when, to my surprise, the shiny red door opened, and a man quickly slipped out and walked straight toward me.

I don't know if I've told you this already, but a witch's intuition is her best weapon, and my intuition at this moment was telling me that this guy was ninety percent pure cockiness. And not the kind which could be fun. Arrogance: it oozed off him. I suppose a man who drives a bright red Lamborghini—worth more than a lot of people earn in their lifetimes—is making a statement.

I quickly took him in. He was probably late-forties, prematurely bald, with the kind of ruddy complexion which suggested that he spent a lot of time in the sun, but his skin had never quite caught the art of tanning. He wore a red polo shirt and, I am not kidding you, it had the Lamborghini logo on it.

I swallowed a groan. This man was a walking cliché.

I'd stake my Rover against his sports car that his keychain had the Lamborghini logo on it, too. His jeans looked more comfortable than stylish, and there was no doubt in my mind that the oversized watch on his wrist was a Rolex. The kind with the most diamonds possible.

In a broad Australian accent, he said, "G'day. Is this where I buy flowers?"

"Good morning," I replied, eking out a smile. "It is indeed."

At least the man was actually here to shop in my store.

His eyes widened slightly. "Ah, so you're not from around these parts, either."

I shook my head. "I'm not."

"I'm from Oz," he said, as though I might not have noticed that fact from the g'day.

"How can I help you?" I did not want to get into a conversation about where we were from and how we liked England. It was a conversation I had too many times a day already. Something about this man made me uncomfortable and, like I said, I'd learned a long time ago to trust my instincts. If he wanted flowers, I would happily sell them to him. And then send him on his way.

I opened the door to my shop and gestured for the man to walk through. I followed him, putting my watering can down behind the counter, where I wrapped flowers and took payments.

He looked around. "Nice place you've got here."

He didn't mention the parrot. People usually mentioned Norman when they walked into my shop. Then I realized that Char's familiar had flown out the open window. I didn't dare look toward the Lamborghini, but I had a bad feeling, a gut feeling of the most unsettling kind. I knew exactly what Norman was doing. He had good instincts about people too, and also a knack for picking up my impressions as well as Char's.

I thanked the man, flashing him another smile, this time hoping that he'd give me an instruction and then our time together could be over.

"I'd like some flowers," he said. His third extremely obvious statement in two minutes.

"Well, you've come to the right place." I could do obvious, too.

He laughed at that as though I were hilarious. "Just bought a little place here," he said. "Old cottage. Thought I'd brighten it up with flowers."

This was news. Unwelcome news. "You bought a place in Willow Waters?"

I kind of hoped he'd say, *Oh, no. Is this Willow Waters? Pardon me thinking I was in Chipping Camden. Sorry about that. I'll be on my way.*

Instead, he said, "Yeah. Sight unseen. Bought it on the Internet."

I couldn't help it, I said, "You bought a house on the Internet?"

"Yeah. Diversifying my interests. I've got a couple of homes in Sydney, a ranch up near Queensland, and a little place in San Francisco. Thought I'd round things out a bit. I made a few bucks. Looking for a nice place to retire."

"I thought people retired to Australia. I think you'll find the weather's a lot better there."

He gave another one of his big guffaws, as though I was doing stand-up. "You're right, can't argue with that, but there are times in life when a man needs a change."

I looked the man over and received the impression that he was running from something. Honestly, I wished he'd just keep on running. Willow Waters is a beautiful and usually quiet village, but there had been some upset lately. We didn't need more trouble.

I did my best to put him off. "It's really quiet here," I told him, leaning forward as though sharing confidences. From the corner of my eye, I could see all the way into the parking area and a flash of blue and yellow, which looked suspiciously parrot-like, hovering over the Lamborghini. Naturally, I didn't turn my head. That would have given the game away.

I was pretty sure there was something drifting down past my vision, sort of like a moth diving toward the car. Go,

Norman! If parrot poop on his fancy car was enough to put this annoying man off living here, I'd be forever grateful.

"There's absolutely nothing to do," I said. "I hope you like peace and quiet." Something about him, like maybe his flashy car, told me he liked nothing less.

"Peace and quiet, huh? Well, it's not what I'm used to, but a little relaxation would set me right up."

"I don't mean to say we don't have any excitement here. We have a weekly pub quiz. And of course, several church services a week. We've recently been blessed with a new vicar. She's quite progressive."

He scratched his chin, and I could see that he'd recently had a manicure. "Don't go in much for preaching." And then it was his turn to look me up and down. "Where would I go if I was going to take a nice lady out for dinner?"

I bristled. Well, I wouldn't be the one going with this guy on a dinner date. However, I cared about tourism and the health of this village too much to lie. "You'd go to The Tudor Rose. It's a historical coaching inn, and the food is fabulous. Or, if you wanted something more casual, all the pubs in the vicinity have good food." I smiled. "All three of them."

"Oh well, I'll see how I go." His phone dinged, and he looked down at it. "Tell you what, dahlin, make me up a nice, big arrangement—no, make that four nice arrangements—and deliver them to Barnham House. I want the best. You get me?"

I tried to resist dropping my jaw. A little cottage? Barnham House was a magnificent Grade I listed former merchant's house, centuries old, situated on several acres of private land. It was famous for its glorious gardens. Every villager and nosy neighbor admired its elegant sweeping driveway, which led to the front of the house. But it was the exquisitely restored gardens surrounding the house—with yew and box topiary and formal lawns and beds—relieved by meadow flower beds and the open fields beyond, which made the home so special. It had been featured in countless magazines and more than one television crew had filmed in the gardens for a period drama.

I hated the idea of this boorish man living there.

It seemed all wrong.

CHAPTER 2

"*W*ill that be enough to get me something nice and cover the delivery? I'm not bothered what you put in the bouquets. Just make them eye-catching." The new owner of Barnham House pulled out his wallet and stripped out eight fifty-pound notes. A hundred pounds per bouquet.

That much money would get him something very nice. Exquisite, maybe. However, the only extra magic that I'd be tempted to put into these four bouquets would be to inspire the buyer with a sudden urge to leave Willow Waters.

"Some of my new furniture's being delivered today, so bring them along this afternoon," he said. As though my schedule was his to dictate.

His phone buzzed again. Without excusing himself, he picked it up.

"Dennis Ratslaff here," he said loudly.

I cannot stand people who do that. Did he think his voice had to carry to Australia? My shop isn't that big, and I swear the leaves on the ferns I use as greenery quivered as he roared his name.

Dennis shot me a thumbs-up as he headed for the door, crossing paths with Vera and her lovely old sheep dog Milton. Vera was a widow, and Milton was her beloved companion. Like the poet he was named for, poor Milton had gone blind in his old age. Also deaf. But he still had his sense of smell and taste and seemed to enjoy his life. He was a sweet boy, and I couldn't imagine how Vera would manage when he passed away. From the look of him, it wouldn't be long. I always kept a few dog treats for him, the soft liver ones for aging canine friends, that were easy on his teeth.

Vera stared at the booming Dennis Ratslaff, who was telling someone on his phone that the deal was still going ahead. He laughed. "Buyer beware, mate. I've got a signed contract. If the fools didn't read it properly, that's on them."

As Dennis continued his annoying conversation outside, Vera greeted me and slowly came closer with her walking stick. She propped it against the side of my counter. Milton perked up when I offered him a liver treat on my open palm, bending down so he could smell it. He took it delicately, wagging his shaggy tail. I murmured a few sweet nothings, stroking his head.

Vera didn't usually buy flowers, as she had a small but pretty garden and her roses were famous, but she liked to come in for a chat, and she knew that Milton was always welcome. I swear that dog had every storekeeper in Willow Waters feeding him treats. He could work the crowd.

However, today Vera surprised me. "Morning, Peony," she said brightly. "Don't you look lovely today?"

I glanced down at my simple denim shirtdress and figured Vera had gotten out of bed on the right side today.

"I'm after a beautiful, *professional* bouquet," she said. "My grandson and his family are coming for a visit. They've just had a baby girl. Rosie, her name is. Isn't that exciting?"

Vera was beaming, her rosy cheeks bright and matching her pink cardigan fastened with mother-of-pearl buttons.

I congratulated Vera on her expanding family and assured her I could arrange a lovely bouquet. We chatted a while about options, though I knew that Vera would eventually settle on something very traditional.

To my surprise, Dennis still hadn't left. "Yeah, call me later," he boomed, then ended the call.

Instead of returning to his precious car, he joined us at the till, where I was writing ideas for flowers with Vera. He glared down at Milton, who ignored him in favor of pointing his nose in my direction, obviously hoping for another treat.

Dennis sniffed hard, his nose wrinkling. If you weren't a dog lover, Milton probably didn't look like much.

"That dog stinks," Dennis said in his obnoxious way. "Shouldn't allow animals in stores."

I opened my mouth to release a cursory telling off, but at that moment Norman swooped in and settled on a handy rafter above Dennis's head. I held my breath, waiting for something unforgivable to happen. But Norman stayed silent. Eerily silent. Fortunately, Dennis didn't notice a thing.

Vera thinned her lips, but didn't respond.

I said, "You won't make friends in Willow Waters if you don't like dogs, Mr. Ratslaff. We're a very dog-friendly community. I would say that almost everyone in these parts is an animal lover."

"Dogs are all right if they're out working, but I got no time for smelly lapdogs. Nasty, flea-ridden things."

Vera ignored the rude Australian with dignity. She simply thanked me and said that she'd pick up Rosie's bouquet later. I was feeling so bad for her after Dennis Ratslaff's rudeness that I offered to deliver her flowers.

"Come, Milton," she said, knowing he couldn't hear her. "We're off to the bakery." She gave his leash a gentle tug, and he obligingly followed.

"That bag of fleas should be put down," Dennis Ratslaff said as the door clicked closed. He shook his head as if Vera had committed some kind of crime against humanity.

I bristled. Had he not heard my earlier warning? But a customer was a customer, after all. I had to remain polite. "Can I help you with something else?"

"Yeah, actually. Got an old girlfriend living round here. Thought I'd send her some flowers."

"You know someone in Willow Waters?" I sounded as surprised as I felt.

"Too right. I grew up in Hartington village, just next door. But I met this bird in Sydney."

I stood still for a moment, stunned at Dennis's admission that he'd grown up nearby. His Australian accent was as thick as Vegemite. But it was more than that. The man had let me chatter on about the quiet charms of the village without once interrupting to say anything about knowing the area. Why?

"No need to look so shocked." He laughed. "I might have the tan of the Aussie gods, but that doesn't mean I'm not a small-town guy. Anyway, I want to send some flowers to Gillian Thompson. You heard of her?" Then he shook his head. "Not Thompson. Gilly got married to some posh bloke who died."

I swallowed. Surely not. "Gillian Fairfax?"

"Is that the name she goes by now? I heard Gilly was recently widowed, and I want to extend my condolences."

Send his condolences, or make his move? It was hard to picture the elegant and slightly uptight Gillian with this geezer. I wondered what it was about Gillian that attracted all these men. Though I suspected her blonde beauty and wealth might have something to do with it. I told Dennis that I knew her and her late husband, Alistair, very well.

He nodded, seemingly pleased, despite the mention of her late husband. "Does she still favor all-white flowers?"

I raised a brow. This was the man who had handed over several fifty-pound notes to decorate his new home without a whiff of interest in the arrangement, but remembered Gillian's preferred bouquet perfectly. Except that Alistair Fairfax had always asked me to add beautiful yellow roses to Gillian's flower arrangements.

I nodded, noncommittal. I didn't exactly want to help this man woo Gillian.

"Gilly loved white freesia when we used to date. I met her when she was modeling in Australia. And I sent her a lot of flowers at that time. Especially toward the end, if you know what I mean."

I couldn't tell if Dennis was acting sheepish or boasting. But my instinct told me that the relationship had not ended well and no prize for guessing whose fault that'd been.

"I'm familiar with Gillian's tastes as well. Her late husband bought her flowers weekly." And take that, Mr. Aussie upstart.

Was that a flash of annoyance across Dennis's face? Between you and me, I hoped so. I didn't like the idea that he thought he could just turn up in Willow Waters and make a play for Gillian. She's been through a lot lately, and although no angel by any means, I sympathized with how difficult it was as an outsider to be accepted by the village.

Dennis pulled out another wad of cash, fingering the notes. No one round here carried that much cash. Or cash at all, really. Everything was on card these days, so why was his wallet so stuffed?

"On second thought," he said, "could you add some Kangaroo Paw? Or Aussie Box? Something to remind Gilly of our time together in Sydney."

I tried not to cringe, then admitted that I didn't have any of those in stock.

"Australian honeysuckle?" he asked hopefully.

I shook my head. "No, but those do smell wonderful."

Dennis looked impatient.

"I have lots of lovely eucalyptus that I know grows in Australia."

He narrowed his eyes. Clearly, this man was used to getting exactly what he wanted. "That will have to do."

"Would you like to include a card or a note?" I asked.

His perplexed frown told me he hadn't considered this addendum. Tactfully, I suggested he might just want to leave his name, a short message of condolence, and let Gillian know he'd returned to Willow Waters. I had a selection of nice cards. Dennis chose not a condolence card, but one that read, *Every Day is a New Beginning.* Then he grabbed the pen from my hand and wrote:

Gilly,

> *Denny's back.*

> *Sorry about recent events.*

> *Let's catch up over a glass of bubbly.*

> *Mwah,*

> *DR*

I found it telling that he didn't add a question mark to his invitation so it read as a command rather than a suggestion. I held back from rolling my eyes and accepted two more fifty-pound notes. Not bad for a morning's work.

"If your flowers are any good," he said, staring down at his phone again, "I'll set up a regular commission, fresh flowers for my new house every week."

Dennis looked up and stood blinking at me, waiting for the expected rush of gratitude. I was torn. He was obviously a potential local client with deep pockets, and Bewitching Blooms needed those to survive, but I didn't like him. I smiled magnanimously and handed him his receipt.

A flutter of feathers from above reminded me that Norman was watching the whole transaction very carefully. Normie was only interested in my customers when they were spilling the beans on some local gossip, and then he liked to jump in with *ooh she never* or *what was he thinking?* But today he remained suspiciously quiet. And I knew why.

I walked with Dennis as he left the store, picking up my watering can where I'd set it down earlier. I glanced up at Normie, who was fluffing his feathers with delight. There was a mischievous glint in his beady eyes.

I opened the door for Dennis and then could barely

contain my mirth as I watched his expression change from smug to seething.

"What is this?" he cried, racing over to his precious Lamborghini.

It was covered in bird poop, of course. White splatterings which began at the hood, creeping over the roof and then down the bumper. Normie had done a thorough job. Obviously, we were feeding him too much.

"How the—?"

Just as Dennis's cursing began to reach obscene levels, the new vicar, Justine Johnson, walked by. She watched him rant and rave with an expression of pure bemusement on her face.

Justine had only been in the village for a couple of weeks, but she already felt like part of the community. At forty-two, she was only a few years older than me, and her relative youth brought with it something fresh and optimistic— exactly what this village needed after the sudden and dramatic departure of our last vicar. She was personable, good-humored, had seemingly endless patience for the long stories many villagers liked to spin, and had a boundless appetite for homemade shortbread—or any sweet treat with which she was presented. This was also a large part of her job.

Dennis paused his rant when he noticed Justine's clerical collar. As if it were her fault, he took a deep breath, glared, and then asked if she could have a word with the big guy upstairs to get pigeons wiped off the face of the earth.

Justine laughed, and her practical brown bob bounced on her broad shoulders. In her deep, plummy voice, she replied, "I'll ask God to take a look at the issue as soon as He has a minute to spare."

Dennis's face was reaching Lamborghini-red levels. Barely a distinction between his polo shirt and his neck remained. He looked skyward and shook his fists at the trees as if they concealed the fugitive poopers. "Bloody pigeons. I'll have you in a pie. Don't you dare!"

He spun back to his car and began inspecting it as tenderly as if it were a newborn baby suffering from a diaper rash. I averted my eyes, afraid I'd laugh.

"My poor baby," he cooed, before turning round and staring at me accusingly. "How did this happen?"

I shrugged benevolently. "The pigeons around this way can be pretty prolific. It's a combination of the pure air and meadows." Maybe the supposed pigeon overpopulation would have him rethinking Willow Waters as a home. I could only hope so.

He looked back at the hood of his car, shaking his head. "These splodges are...enormous! I've never seen anything like it. Not even koalas expel this much waste, and those critters eat all day long."

"As I said, it's all this fresh Cotswold air," I proffered. "Might be something you have to get used to around here. Although I must say we do all view it as a benefit, not a drawback." I flashed him a small smile.

Dennis grimaced. He muttered something about pigeon poop being corrosive and having to call his car dealership before sliding behind the driving seat and zooming off. The ferocious sound of his engine rang in my ears as I watched him break the speed limit along our quiet high street.

"Speedy Gonzalez over there really must keep an eye out for pigeons," Normie said slyly, as he flew down to land on one of my flower baskets. "And seagulls, crows, robins, whatever's around."

"Quite," the vicar said, laughing. Luckily, she had a great sense of humor.

Norman did take some getting used to, but it seemed as if Justine was accepting him as just another aspect of the local color. I wondered if she had guessed the true origin of Dennis's dismay and was too polite to point it out.

It was one of the rare occasions where I didn't feel the need to chastise Normie. In fact, while the vicar peered at the window display, I held up a hand for a high five. He fanned out his colorful right wing, and we grinned at each other.

"I'll have you in a pie. Don't you dare!" Normie parroted Dennis perfectly.

I giggled, and the vicar joined in.

"Never a dull moment when you're around," she said affectionately.

I was glad the vicar had taken to Norman. He was a divisive figure in the village. Some people loved him. Others... Well, let's just say they found him a nuisance. I knew which category Dennis would shove him into when he finally worked out that a parrot ruled these skies.

"Right, that's enough work for one morning," Normie said, yawning. "Time for a nap." He flew back to his favorite perch in my shop.

The vicar gazed after him and then back at my blooms. "Your hanging baskets are quite lovely," she said, lightly touching the rattan basket.

I glowed. They *did* look rather lovely at this time of year. There's nothing quite as captivating as a store entrance flanked by a pair of exuberantly overflowing hanging baskets. This year I'd gone heavy on the color and texture and scent to attract as many passers-by as possible. Fuchsias, petunias, nasturtiums, verbena, and trailing ivy led your eye toward my front door. If my baskets could talk, they'd say: "Go in, it's delightful, feast your eyes and unburden your wallets." But then I'd have the problem of chatty flowers, and a chatty parrot was quite enough for one store.

The roar of an accelerating engine traveled across the breeze. Dennis really needed to slow down. Just because a car could break the sound barrier didn't mean it had to every time the man went out for a pint of milk.

The vicar raised her eyebrows at me. "What *was* that all about? Was that gentleman just passing through?"

If only. I told Justine the background info I'd gleaned about Willow Waters' latest addition. Suffice to say that her eyebrows stayed high on her forehead. Willow Waters often attracted the wealthy, but not the ostentatious.

But true to her calling, the vicar didn't pass judgment on Dennis. Instead, she wondered how he might help the village. "Do you think he might be interested in donating to help preserve our lovely old church? We're in desperate need of repairs and right now our funds are short. I don't suppose you got the sense that he's Anglican?" She let out a short laugh, and her hair swung. "Or I am being overly optimistic?"

I thought back to how Dennis said he didn't much go in for preaching. "Maybe if you rid the world of pigeons, he'll convert?" I suggested.

"I have enough trouble keeping the spiders out of my bathroom," she replied.

I smiled. I could just imagine Justine trying to shepherd a

spider out of her tub and into the garden. "Tell me, how are you settling in, Vicar?" I asked.

"Who couldn't love a place like Willow Waters?" she replied, beaming. "Though I must admit that it's taking time for the villagers to get used to me. We all have our own way of doing things. The former vicar's ways are not mine."

Now it was my turn to raise a brow. Surely it was a blessing that the new vicar strayed far from the ways of the old. But then again, it all came back to the village's slow pace. No one here embraced change, and it would take a while for them to accept Justine as one of their own, even if they were perfectly pleasant to her in the meantime.

It had taken me long enough to become an accepted member of this community, and I recalled how much it had bothered me. I wasn't like my spirit-medium mother, Jessie Rae, who cared nothing for fitting in—would, in fact, much rather *not* fit in. Or Char, who considered herself a rebel (even if it was without a cause). And with that thought, I realized that Justine would fit in quite perfectly with my motley little crew of women at the farmhouse—as long as none of them mentioned witchcraft, of course. Char and my mom were used to keeping their witchiness a secret from my housemate, Hilary, so I'd have to trust they'd be well-behaved for the vicar, too.

"Vicar, would you be free this weekend to join us for dinner at my farmhouse? It's a ten-minute drive from here. I have two boarders who live with me, Hilary and Char—and my mom, who may as well do—and we often eat dinner together. It would be so nice for you to meet them all."

The vicar beamed. "That would be quite lovely. Thank you, Peony."

"Saturday evening, if you're free?"

The vicar nodded. "My calendar isn't exactly jam-packed yet."

"But I'm sure the parishioners are supplying you with enough jam. Am I right?"

She lowered her voice, though there was no one else in the store. "The kitchen shelves are *full*. Elizabeth Sanderson, the head of the Women's Institute, has given me three pots of blackberry alone. I haven't the heart to tell anyone I don't like jam."

"Very wise. The WI mean well."

I dashed inside for a notecard to jot down my address and then handed it over.

She stared at the card for a moment and then back at me. I blinked, waiting.

Justine said, "With all that pigeon drama I'd almost forgotten why I'd come here." She explained how she'd been asked by the WI to head a panel of judges for a friendly prettiest-garden competition. "I was hoping, what with all your flower expertise, that you might come on board as a fellow judge? You seemed like the perfect choice to me."

"Of course," I said quickly. I was flattered. And I loved gardens! Now I'd be able to tour the nicest ones in the area without feeling like a snoop. It was perfect.

"Wonderful. I'll add you to my panel of judges. Let's hope the competition isn't too cutthroat."

CHAPTER 3

$\mathcal{T}$he vicar soon fell into conversation with Bernard Drake. Bernard was a former music teacher and now the church's organ player. To my mind, he was one of the nicest folks in Willow Waters.

Our high street was like that. We were always bumping into each other in Roberto's, or coming and going from our local shops. Bernard and Justine were chatting, probably about church business, when a car (this one going much slower than Dennis Ratslaff's, thank goodness) drove down the high street and pulled into my customer parking spot that Dennis had recently vacated.

Ranya Gupta, one of the booking agents who looked after some of the holiday lettings in the village, stepped out. I was happy to see her, as she was always cheerful and loved flowers almost as much as I did. Together, we went inside, and I helped her choose three of our ready-made bouquets to place in hallways as a welcoming touch for new clients arriving for a long weekend.

Normally, we had advance notice to prepare flowers for

the holiday lets, but these had been last-minute bookings. I worked hard to keep the agents happy. They were an important part of my business. Ranya's company had an account with us, so I charged the purchases and helped carry the bouquets to her car.

You might not be surprised to hear that the 'pigeons' had left Ranya's vehicle alone.

She drove away, and I was about to go back inside when I saw a now-familiar Lamborghini approaching.

Dennis Ratslaff's red car zoomed around the corner and onto the high street at breakneck speed. What was that man up to? Did he simply want everyone in the village to be alerted to his presence? But his driving was beyond just drawing attention to himself. It was reckless.

I glanced ahead. Justine and Bernard were still chatting, some tourists were snapping photos of the street, and then I saw Vera and Milton.

What happened next unfurled in slow motion like a scene from the movies.

Vera was trying to balance her paper bag from the bakery in the same hand as Milton's lead. With her other hand, she leaned heavily on her walking stick and stepped off the curb to cross the road. Milton was on a long lead and, unable to hear anything, plodded on ahead.

The Lamborghini raced toward Milton. But the poor sweet dog was completely oblivious.

Vera dropped her bakery bag and yanked on Milton's lead as she hobbled toward him. "Milton!" she called out in vain. There was no way she'd be able to move fast enough to reach him.

My magic wasn't strong enough to stop a speeding car,

but oh, I wanted to stop the tragedy unfolding in front of my eyes.

Bernard and the vicar turned and then at the same time, the three of us broke into a run.

"Stop," Justine yelled, but it was obvious the man in the speeding car couldn't hear her.

I didn't want to look, but I couldn't avert my eyes as the red sports car sped toward the oblivious old dog.

At the last possible second, the driver swerved, leaving an inch between the fender and the dog. I swear the air current lifted Milton's fur as the car sped by. Milton froze on the road, blinking and panting. The poor sweetheart had obviously sensed that something was wrong.

Dennis slowed long enough to open his window. But instead of an apology, he yelled, "Keep your filthy mutt off the road!" and closed the window again.

And then the most peaceful woman in Willow Waters raised her walking stick and struck the back of the Lamborghini as it drove away. She shook her stick after him. "You won't get away with this, you dreadful man!"

But I doubt he even heard her. He was already speeding away.

Vera dropped her stick to kneel and take Milton into her arms. She cooed to the sweet dog, who snuggled into her embrace and licked her face, unaware of his near-miss with death.

"What an evil thing to do," Bernard said, shaking his head as he watched the road where Dennis had raced off.

A tall, broad-shouldered man about the vicar's age sprinted up the road. He was wearing smart navy trousers and a white shirt and had a head of premature salt-and-pepper hair.

Bernard pointed in his direction and said, "Ah, good. That's Vera's grandson, Neil. He'll soon have her feeling better."

I'd never met any of Vera's family before, and I was glad they were here when she most needed comfort. Neil helped his grandmother to her feet, and the vicar restored her walking stick to her.

"What happened here?" Neil asked. "We were just stopping for coffee when we saw you from the window." He gestured behind him to a beautiful, dark-haired woman who was pushing a pram up the street.

Vera was still too upset to talk, so Bernard relayed Dennis's terrible behavior.

Neil's expression dropped, and all the love he had for his grandmother flowed from his body. He gazed at the now empty street.

"Who behaves like that?" he asked. "Terrify a poor old dog and upset an old woman?"

I decided there and then that before I delivered Vera's bouquet, I'd imbue it with a little magic to bring comfort to the house and fill Neil and his new young family with the desire to return often. It struck me again how lonely Vera would be once Milton was gone.

With Vera safely in the care of her family, the small group which had gathered on the side of the street disbanded.

And then I had an idea. If I wanted to know more about Dennis Ratslaff, and I did, Bernard might be able to help. He'd lived in the village all his life. I wondered if he would remember Dennis. I was finding it impossible to imagine the arrogant and aggressive Australian coming from this sleepy part of the world. And there was something about his story that didn't sit right with me.

I asked Bernard if he'd have a moment, and the two of us headed back toward Bewitching Blooms. Bernard crossed the road carefully, looking from right to left and then left to right before stepping out despite there being no traffic to speak of. Clearly, Dennis had gotten to him as well.

I'd learned to read something of people's auras from my mother, Jessie Rae, who was a medium. Bernard's aura was a true, light pink—a rarity. The color represented a gentle soul, and he radiated a pleasant, loving energy. For the first time, I thought about how he and my mom might get along, but immediately retracted the thought—Jessie Rae would eat poor Bernard for breakfast.

Bernard was wearing his usual uniform of tweed trousers and golfing top that paid no heed to the seasons. His gray hair was wispy, and the morning's breeze whipped a few strands across his head. He had two parcels wrapped in brown paper tucked under his arm, which I hadn't noticed before now. "I'm on my way to the post office, so I'll walk with you to your shop. What can I help you with, Peony?"

"I wanted to ask you a local history question," I said, thinking on my feet regarding the best way to avoid sounding nosy.

Bernard's light eyes flashed. He stopped walking and turned to me. "A favorite topic of mine. We've a very interesting history here in Willow Waters. Why, in 1646 the Royalists marched through this very village hoping to meet up with the king in Oxford. That's during the civil war, of course, when Charles II was fighting to regain the throne from

Cromwell. But goodness me, we can go much earlier than that. The Romans occupied this part of the world two thousand years ago." He motioned to the street we were still standing beside. "Why, this very road was built by the Romans. Lovely straight roads they designed. In fact, there are Roman remains all through the Cotswolds."

Before he took me back to the Neolithic age, I hastily interrupted him.

"I'm curious about something much more modern than that." I hesitated. "Did you recognize the man in the Lamborghini?"

Bernard shook his head. "No, I didn't get a close enough look. Everything happened in such a blur."

I explained that he'd been a rather unusual customer of mine this morning. I managed to sum him up in one pithy sentence, "He's an Australian fast-talking, deal-making ex-Cotswold resident with pockets deep enough to snap up Barnham House." Okay, maybe it wasn't that pithy.

"Barnham House?" Bernard looked shocked, as well he might. "I'd heard it sold. Are you saying that horrible man who nearly killed poor old Milton is the new owner?"

"Yup. On top of everything, he bought the house on the Internet. Sight unseen. Though maybe it wasn't sight unseen, as he told me he's originally from here."

"That man was brought up locally?" He seemed appalled that any Cotswold parent would raise a dog-hater.

I told him the Lamborghini owner was in the store at the same time as Vera and Milton and was extremely rude to them both. "So, imagine my surprise when he told me that he was actually from this area. His name is Dennis Ratslaff. Do you remember anyone by that name?"

Bernard's kind face darkened. "Dennis Ratslaff is back? I'd hoped we'd seen the last of him."

My intuition had been right. There was something seriously amiss with this newcomer. Or oldcomer, as it turned out.

"So you do know him? I didn't warm to him," I confessed, "even before the dog incident."

"I should think not. I'm surprised he would even show his face around here, let alone buy a much-cherished historical property."

I flashed Bernard an encouraging look—a 'your secrets are safe with me' look.

"It's a long and frankly quite dreadful story." He paused, taking a dramatic breath. "Dennis Ratslaff made himself famous around these parts—for all the wrong reasons. Many moons ago, he ran a dodgy scheme with used cars. His motto was *buyer beware*. He never cared if the car fell apart after it was sold. He felt it was the fault of the buyer to be so gullible."

"That's terrible!" I said, enraged. If there was one thing I knew about running a local business, it was that you were nothing without loyal customers. And that loyalty had to be earned with honesty, fair dealings, and customer service.

Bernard nodded. "And downright dangerous. A young chap in the village named Ralph Dawson suffered the worst of Dennis's scheme. Ralph bought one of the dodgy cars and after a couple of months, the brakes went. The car broke through a fence and went right through a window into his family's front room."

I gasped.

"Luckily, no one was hurt," Bernard added quickly.

"Ralph swore the brakes were faulty, but Dennis said they were working when he sold the car. Ralph's insurance premiums went way up, and his house was never quite the same with the replacement window and the loss of the ancient roses that grew around it."

"How dreadful."

"Ralph tried to get the police involved, but Dennis upped sticks and moved away. No one knew where to."

"Australia," I offered helpfully.

Bernard looked glum. "Dennis ripped a lot of people off and caused some accidents that could have ended in tragedy. He made many enemies, and people have long memories. I'm surprised he has the gall to show his face around here again."

Didn't it just figure that a guy who got his start selling unreliable second-hand cars was now driving one of the most expensive, best-engineered cars in the world? It seemed he'd become very wealthy in the years since he'd left Willow Waters. In the brief time we'd spent together, he'd mentioned properties in Sydney, a ranch near Queensland, and a 'little place' in San Francisco.

"He bought Barnham House to *retire* in," I told Bernard.

His eyebrows shot up. "Why, that man can't be more than forty-five. How can the fellow be *retiring*?"

"Beats me," I said. But somehow I doubted he'd amassed a fortune in any respectable profession.

Bernard looked perplexed. He opened his mouth to speak and then closed it again.

"What is it?" I asked, as innocently as I could.

"I'm not one for gossip," Bernard said carefully, "but a rotten car dealership isn't the only thing Dennis left behind when he took off." He shot me a knowing look. "He was quite the womanizer."

And now Dennis Ratslaff was sending flowers to Gillian Fairfax. No doubt Bernard would have welcomed that bit of gossip, but I kept my mouth shut.

If there was one thing I'd learned as a flower shop owner, it was the importance of confidentiality. My customers bought flowers for all occasions—and often their purchases were fueled by grief, anger, and regret, as well as celebration and love. As a florist, I sometimes witnessed customers' raw emotions. And although my job made me privy to many a private matter in the village, I would never betray what I learned about my neighbors. A good florist was as discreet as a doctor or a therapist. I had no idea what was between Dennis and Gillian, but I hoped, for her sake, she would leave the romantic past in the past.

I told Bernard it was nice to talk and that I'd see him in The Mermaid for quiz night this week. He dipped his head ever so slightly and headed toward the post office. I watched as he disappeared in the same direction Dennis had gone. Something told me that I hadn't seen the last of Mr. Ratslaff this week.

CHAPTER 4

*T*he rest of the morning passed peacefully. Thursday afternoons were always a busy time for me at the shop, as this was when lots of people liked to order their weekend flowers or pop into the store to browse.

Imogen arrived and we got into the flow of a busy day. After several years as colleagues, we had found a good rhythm. I appreciated her artistry, even if I thought she could be too much of a perfectionist. She'd accepted that I was willing to try new things to grow the business and that my less than perfect arrangements had their place. I'd go so far as to say we even appreciated our differences, and these were the basis for us becoming closer. When I put down my scissors halfway through cutting ribbon for a bouquet to answer the phone, Imogen picked them up automatically, and when I returned from my call, the bouquet was neatly tied with a perfect bow. It was nice.

Imogen was also a fountain of Willow Waters' knowledge. Born and bred in the village, after a couple of years at a top floral design company in London, she'd decided that city life wasn't for her and returned home. Lucky for me, not only did I appreciate her talents, but I could also dive into that local knowledge when needed—which seemed to be more and more these days.

When she arrived, I immediately asked her about Dennis Ratslaff, of course, but Imogen told me that any scandal was before her time. Sometimes I forget she's only twenty-four. After I told her how he'd nearly killed poor Milton and upset Vera, she was suitably horrified and said that she would ask her parents later.

For now, I figured the best way to suss out Willow Waters' newest resident was to deliver his flowers myself.

Imogen and I had done a wonderful job on the bouquets. We prided ourselves on consistently good arrangements, no matter the client, and as I did our books, I also knew that we needed the kind of client who had deep pockets and would think nothing of setting up a healthy standing order.

So, I'd deliver his flowers. I suspected he'd notice that the shop owner delivered his bouquets herself, and that would matter to him. He'd always want what he perceived to be the best service.

"Just one more," Imogen called out from the storefront as I rearranged the blooms in the back of my Range Rover.

Norman flapped over. "Just one little poop?" he croaked, nodding at one of our beautiful bouquets.

"You've done quite enough of that for one day," I chastised. "You stay clear of my flowers."

Norman let out an evil cackle, but obeyed my instruction. That bird knew which way his bread was buttered. Or his seeds were scattered. You catch my drift.

Imogen staggered over with a huge bouquet which held

the last of Dennis's order. We had gone with quite a flamboyant bright and sunny look, aiming to bring some of the magic of the gardens at Barnham inside the house. Speaking of which...

I waited until Imogen had gone back inside and then thought about imbuing the blooms with some magic. Ordinarily, I strengthened the natural uplifting properties of flowers with well-wishes, but with Dennis, I was very tempted to cast a spell which would make him want to leave. I stared hard at our arrangements. Fresh and pretty bouvardia, white lilac, and paper-white narcissus. Summer meadow-inspired Sanguisorba, clematis, delphiniums, white dill, lilac, Memory Lane and Bounty Way roses paired with grasses and spirea. A third and more herbaceous mix of flowering mint, cleansing sage, sea oats grasses, pale-blue mini delphinium, pale-blue nigella, and perfectly dainty rice flowers.

We had covered several of our signature styles and showed off our joint talents. Could I really use such beautiful blooms as a vehicle for getting someone to leave town? No. It was important that my dislike of the man didn't cross-pollinate with magic. And I knew that the effects of any negative magic could twist and mutate, coming back twice as potent and in a direction all of its own.

I decided instead to change my spell to one of calmness and good decisions. Maybe a positive influence was all Dennis needed to quell his temper and become a good citizen.

Quietly, I spoke the words of my spell.

"Begone, all worry and woe!

Break free from anger and gain the wisdom to grow
Take life slow
Allow your calm to grow
Serenity and tranquility will then overflow."

I smiled at the words *take life slow* and wondered if Dennis had managed to get the parrot poop off his car. I'd rather he was washing it than using it to terrorize innocent people and dogs.

I waved to Norman, told him not to make a nuisance of himself for Imogen while I was gone, and set off for Barnham House.

The old manor house was on the outskirts of the village, not far from where Vera and Milton lived, sadly for them, and on the other side of the woodlands where Alex Stanford's grand castle stood. Speaking of which…I guess you might be wondering a bit about Alex and me after our non-date dinner the other week, but we'll come to that in time. Just be patient.

Where was I? Oh yes. The drive to Dennis's was longer than my usual delivery time, but on such a gorgeous day I didn't mind. The windows were wound down and a fresh breeze rushed into my Range Rover as I sang along to the radio.

I don't think I've told you this before, but I find singing in the car so relaxing. Nowhere else, mind you. I wouldn't want to inflict that torture on some innocent bystander, but belting along to a ballad as I carefully wound my way round the Cotswold lanes was a treat. It was a pleasure to watch the trees and meadows go by, and I instantly felt soothed by being surrounded by nature.

In fact, I felt so good that only then did I realize how

much tension I'd been holding in my body. Why had Dennis gotten to me so much? Yes, he was abrupt, smug, and downright rude to Vera. Yes, Bernard's talk of Dennis's dodgy car business got my back up. But if I was honest with myself, I was feeling strangely protective of Gillian.

I can hear you groaning, and I'll be the first to say that I'd never really warmed to Gillian Fairfax. She was haughty, groomed to within an inch of her life, and let's just say a little problematic in the romance department of her life. But since she'd been widowed, I finally saw the softer, more vulnerable side to Gillian. She was lonely in Willow Waters, and although she hadn't always been the most trustworthy of neighbors, she wasn't the she-devil that many people around here liked to make out. She'd joined the WI to make friends, but the women were still keeping her at arm's length.

She was going to have to regain people's trust, and I didn't think a relationship with Dennis Ratslaff was the best way to do that. Besides, he'd hinted pretty strongly that he'd treated her badly, so I wasn't so sure she'd welcome the bouquet we were set to send on his behalf. If anything, it might reopen old wounds. And everyone had the right to move on with their life. I knew that better than anyone.

Before long, I'd reached Barnham House. I'd driven by many times, but never been inside. The house had stunned me when Jeremy and I first moved to Willow Waters, and it stunned me now.

Mature hornbeam hedges flanked the elegant, sweeping driveway, leading the eye toward the main façade of the house, which was baroque yet relatively simple. Built from the same brick as the other ancient houses in the neighborhood, this one particularly shone. It was five bays wide and three stories high, with three Dutch gables at its apex. Four very tall chimneys and twelve stacks gave this fabulous building its crown, along with a clay peg-tile roof.

Yes, I knew terms like peg-tile roof, which means it's covered with handmade clay tiles. And yes, they're expensive. It's amazing what you find out when you start renovating an ancient farmhouse you call home.

I pulled in to the long drive, parked, and took a closer look. But any sense of tranquility was interrupted by the sound of profuse swearing. I followed it and found Dennis to the side of his new home, furiously washing the last splodges of bird poop off his car.

I was surprised that he was tackling the job himself. Surely Dennis was the kind to pay someone to do his dirty work for him? But then again, maybe he was a control freak and didn't trust anyone else with his red baby.

"Bloody pigeons," Dennis said when he saw me approaching.

"Real pests," I offered half-heartedly. "I've come with your flowers."

Dennis straightened and smoothed down his red polo shirt, which was now flecked with soap suds. "You deliver the flowers yourself?"

"Of course," I said. "We mostly do all our own deliveries. It's a small village, as I said, and our customers prefer the more personal touch."

"But you're the owner, right, dahlin? You don't have, like, any underlings to do the dirty work?"

I stiffened like my familiar Blue when she spied one of the farmhouse's many rogue mice. "I don't consider *any* work to be dirty," I replied emphatically. "Unless you're quite literally plowing a field." I reminded myself that I wanted this horrible man's business and smiled. "But I only do deliveries myself to our most important clients."

As I'd suspected, thinking he was getting extra special treatment immediately worked on his massive ego.

"Since you've driven all the way out here, I suppose you'll be wanting a tour of the house."

As much as I did want a peek inside his famous house, I also didn't want to give him the wrong impression. I wasn't here to see Dennis. I'd have to be all business first.

I explained that I'd love to but would need to unload the flowers first. He nodded and followed me back to my car.

"Ah, now these are something mega," he said, grinning, as I showed him our work. "Fresh and lovely, but cool, too. I like, I like."

"I'm glad," I said, allowing myself to accept the compliment. I meant it. Any good review of our work paid dividends.

"Lemme give you a hand," he said, as if he were doing me the greatest favor in the world. "A little lass like you shouldn't be straining your back."

Hmm, if only Dennis knew quite how powerful I was, then he'd think twice about being patronizing. I swallowed down a retort and followed Dennis into the massive house.

"Put them wherever you think," he said, then gestured at a huge sideboard. "I'll have one there."

Behind his back, I rolled my eyes but placed the flowers where he'd pointed. Normally, we'd tie the bouquets with little water pouches, but I'd decided to throw in four plain vases. They weren't expensive, and I felt that Dennis would be more likely to reorder if he had empty vases to deal with.

The sideboard had to be as old as the house, made of

carved oak. "Should I put a plate underneath or something? The vase could be damp."

He seemed unconcerned. "I bought the house furnished. I wouldn't give houseroom to most of this old junk, but it'll get me started."

Old junk? I glanced around the entrance hall. It was stunning. An enormous grandfather clock ticked grandly away. There was a low marble-topped table—flanked by carved chairs—on the other side of the hall. I placed a second bouquet on there. I still had two more arrangements.

"Perhaps one in the dining room and one in the lounge?" I suggested.

But he paid no heed. "Whatever. Come and have the tour. You'll be my first official visitor." He threw out his arms and said, "Welcome to my humble *casa*. I'd say *mi casa* is *su casa*, but I don't think we know each other well enough for that...yet."

Light streamed in through the four tall box-sash windows through which I could see the formal gardens which made this lovely house so famous. To the rear was a handsome staircase.

"The library is down that way," Dennis said, shrugging, as if to say who'd need a library in their home. "The dining hall is on the other side." He walked toward that room and opened the door, beckoning for me to follow.

I could tell by his erect posture that Dennis was especially pleased with the dining room. And who wouldn't be? It had seventeenth-century oak paneling and an exquisite, molded plaster ceiling. Under my feet were Purbeck flagstones. I'd priced them for my farmhouse, and let's just say I'd have to sell a lot of flowers to afford anything similar.

Two open fireplaces were at either end of the room, but its centerpiece was a glorious antique dining table, truly fit for a king and queen.

"This room is very special," I said as I placed one of the arrangements in the middle of the table.

"Probably a little smaller than I'll be needing," he said. "Of course, I'll be installing underfloor heating, so some of this flagstone will have to go. And that hideous table."

I turned in surprise. No, in horror. "But the table is breathtaking," I said. "It looks like it was made bespoke for this very room."

Dennis shrugged again. "I thought I might put the snooker table in here, actually."

I burst out laughing.

"What?" Dennis asked. "You don't play snooker? It's great. I'll teach you."

He wasn't joking. Oh dear, I was going to need all my professional patience for this one.

He led me out of the dining room to the kitchen at the back of the house. "It's connected now, but the agent told me that the cook's house was traditionally detached from the main house for safety."

I nodded, too busy taking in the kitchen's details to listen to Dennis's narration. I immediately spotted original bread ovens, marble worktops, and open shelves dotted among the tall, arched beams. "There's so many original features intact," I breathed. It was this kind of house which had sent me head-first in love with Willow Waters in the first place.

Another infuriating shrug from Dennis. "It's a good size, but I'll have all this old rubbish ripped out and a new kitchen put in."

I wanted to chain myself to the old bread oven in protest. "You know this is a Grade I listed building? You have to get permission for changes," I said.

"Man's home is his castle," was his reply.

I followed in a desirous daze as we walked beneath soaring ceilings with their graphic lines of blackened timbers. Every room was elegant, flooded with light, and yet the architectural features of the original building had never been compromised. It was a masterclass in sensitive restoration, and I wanted to get back to my own interior-design scrapbooks immediately.

I put the fourth bouquet in a big front room with beautiful antiques he'd no doubt be throwing away so he could put something plastic and garish in their place.

We returned to the grand hall.

"There's a wine cellar, of course," Dennis said. "Soon to be filled with my collection of Australian vintages, which are winging their way to this side of the planet as we speak. Did I mention I own a vineyard? And loads of bedrooms upstairs."

"It's beautiful," I said. "Could I get a look at the famous gardens here?"

"Oh, you're interested in gardens, are you? Not really my bag. But be my guest." He opened one of several side doors, and we stepped out into the sunshine and onto golden sand pathways which formed a network around the formal lawns.

Here was the famously tended box hedging and topiary designs, mature evergreens towering above us. I cooed at the rose and flower borders, lavender gardens, and orchard. There was also a large pond, with a small island, and woodland beyond. I couldn't believe how beautiful it all was. So secluded and luscious.

"You're a lucky man, Dennis," I said.

"All the product of hard work," he said. "No luck about it."

Wow, did this man ever let up with the boasting?

Closer to the house was an old kitchen garden where I could smell herbs, and beside that was a seating area with comfortable-looking rattan furniture where I could imagine enjoying a cup of tea and a book. But something on the house wall behind the seating area caught my eye. I stepped closer to get a better look and gasped. Rows of long spears were fixed to the brick wall!

Dennis turned. "Aha! I see you're admiring my collection of Aboriginal hunting spears. Beauties, aren't they?"

It wasn't a question I wanted to answer. What I did want to know was why he'd put them on the outside of his new, Grade I listed house. No, scrub that. What on earth was he doing with a collection of Aboriginal hunting spears in the first place? Had the man not heard of cultural appropriation?

"I'm amazed you were able to import them," I said.

"Had some trouble, you're right. Got them into the country as works of art." He stared at the lethal-looking spears. "Had to pull down some pesky clematis to get a bare wall on this place, but now everyone who visits will see I mean business."

Personally, I thought Dennis had no business at all with the spears. They didn't belong to him, not really. You couldn't just buy your way into another culture's ancestry. And he had no right using them to intimidate guests.

He seemed oblivious to my discomfort and continued with the tour. "I'm thinking of putting the pool house in there," he said, pointing at a lovely flint cottage on the outer edges of the grounds, which would have once belonged to the groundskeeper.

"Pool house?" I asked faintly. "But it's so close to the wildflower meadow."

But Dennis scoffed and wrinkled his sunburned nose. "That bunch of overgrown weeds? I'm going to have the lot of it dug up to put in a swimming pool. Olympic size so I can do my laps. And some palm trees. Give this place the tropical treatment."

I couldn't believe what I was hearing. "You're not," I said, hoping this was some kind of weird joke, but knowing deep down that Dennis was deadly serious.

"Willow Waters needs to be dragged into the twenty-first century. And I'm gonna be the one to do it."

I gasped. "But this is a listed home. The grounds included. Are you sure you're even allowed to do that?"

Dennis laughed. "Easier to ask forgiveness than permission, dahlin. Don't tell the curtain-twitchers, but the digger's coming tomorrow."

CHAPTER 5

I swallowed hard, straining to contain how appalled I felt.

I told Dennis it was time I was going, and he saw me out. But as he opened the door, a man was standing there, his hand raised to knock.

"Oh," the man said in a polite voice, "hello there. I'm Arthur Higginsbottom, the head of the local historical society here in Willow Waters."

Arthur Higginsbottom was a little portly and looked to be in his early fifties, with strands of gray hair combed to one side. His eyebrows were much darker, reddish, and quite bushy. His face was red too, though whether it was from a condition or embarrassment was hard to discern. He was wearing a crumpled brown suit with a pale-yellow shirt, the top two buttons undone—all slightly loose to give the impression that the man had shrunk since their purchase.

"I was hoping to meet with the new owner of Barnham House?" he added.

"That's me," Dennis said proudly, clapping a hand to his chest. "Guilty as charged." He let out a tremendous guffaw.

Arthur looked a little taken aback but murmured, "Marvelous," and extended a hand to shake.

Dennis grasped it and pumped it with vigor.

I noticed then that Arthur's other hand was clutching a book. I tilted my head to read the title and saw it was a book of local history.

"The society sent me to talk you through the history of your beautiful new home." He presented Dennis with the book. "There's even a special chapter in here on Barnham House. We're very much hoping you'll follow in your predecessor's steps and have open days at the house. It has so much local history." Arthur was beaming, seemingly unperturbed that Dennis had not yet invited him in.

"Right," Dennis said, making no motion to take the book.

It hung suspended between the two men.

Talk about awkward.

Arthur cleared his throat and looked hopefully past Dennis's shoulder, obviously waiting to be invited in.

"History isn't really my bag, yah know? Everything in it is *dead*."

Arthur inhaled sharply. "Sir, I—" He faltered. Clearly Arthur had never encountered someone so history-adverse.

"I'd love to take a look at your book," I said quickly, stepping away from the door to stand beside Arthur. I'd had just about enough of Dennis's abrasive attitude for one day. No, scrap that. For a lifetime. "I'm Peony Bellefleur, the owner of Bewitching Blooms. I'm sure I've seen you around, Mr. Higginsbottom, but we've never formally met."

"Yeah, show the broad," Dennis said. "She'll love it." His

phone began to ring. "Must get this," he said, and turned away, dismissing the pair of us.

Arthur said, "I don't think I've been spoken to so abruptly since my housemaster at boarding school scolded me for not returning my library books on time."

"That seems to be his default mode of communication." We reached my Range Rover, and I looked around for Arthur's vehicle. "Did you walk here?"

"Indeed. It was a lovely afternoon for a stroll, though the atmosphere has soured somewhat, I must say."

I had an idea and asked Arthur if he'd like a lift back to the village center. He accepted graciously. As casually as I could muster, I mentioned that Dennis had already rubbed a few Willowers up the wrong way.

Arthur sighed. "I wish Mr. Ratslaff would have heard me out. The Historical Society was thrilled when Barnham House finally sold. It had been empty too long, and no one was there to water the gardens and maintain the building, so some of our members were doing so voluntarily. It's so, so important to preserve historical houses. Too many people want to rip the old things out and replace them with modern structures and luxuries. But at what cost? When we lose history, we lose part of ourselves. That part is irreplaceable. It's our origin story."

It was so nice to listen to someone passionate about their interests.

I lowered the Rover's windows and put it into gear. But before I began to drive, I turned and looked at Arthur Higginsbottom. Observing his serious, stricken expression, I considered the impact of what I was about to say. But there were no two ways about it. Dennis had to be stopped.

So I took a breath and told Arthur that Dennis was planning to dig up the historic garden. "He told me in confidence, but it's not a confidence I feel obliged to keep."

"Goodness gracious," Arthur managed to splutter.

I got the impression it was the worst curse he'd muttered in decades.

As I was about to pull out, I heard shouts of fury. Arthur and I swiveled in our seats. The freshly washed Lamborghini was splattered with poop again. Norman! I looked around the drive and spotted that cheeky parrot perched on the branch of a mature oak tree. Dennis's enemies in Willow Waters weren't all human.

Dennis's complexion was as red as his car again. He stormed over to the nearest tree and shook his fist. "I'll get you pigeons. Every tree, every bush, everything you could perch on will be gone. You hear me? Scorched earth. That's all that will be left. Then you can go do your business somewhere else."

Dennis was so toxic; I couldn't drive off fast enough. But as I exited the driveway, I heard a terrible squawking.

"You not going to offer me a ride, doll, after I do all your dirty work for you?" Norman said shrilly, like I'd left my wet towels on the bathroom floor. He flew through my open window and into the back seat.

Arthur Higginsbottom was still in shock. He didn't seem to notice that a talking parrot had appeared, which was fine by me—I did get tired of explaining Normie's antics to the uninitiated.

"We can do something, right?" I asked, hoping for some reassurance. "About preserving the wildflowers?"

"Of course, what Mr. Ratslaff is planning to do is illegal.

But if he digs it up before we get the paperwork together...
Well, then we've lost the battle before it's even begun."

"That can't happen!" I exclaimed.

"We'll think of something," Arthur said firmly. "We have to. I'll go straight to my colleagues at the Historical Society. One of them is a retired barrister."

"Slap him with the law!" Normie squeaked. "Before it's too late."

~

BACK AT THE STORE, with Normie safely ensconced on his favorite perch, the full shock of Dennis's plans to destroy the famous gardens at his new abode hit me. It really was the epitome of egotism to disregard something so historic for his own selfish desires. Didn't that man have enough already? How much could one person really own?

"It's been a busy afternoon," Imogen relayed, retying her long, swinging ponytail. "But I finished Gillian's flowers. If it's okay with you, after locking up, I'll deliver them on my way home this evening?" She lifted the bouquet.

"Oh, it's lovely!" The arrangement had a whimsical feel, with a romantic, looser shape and an abundance of white billowing blooms set against the fragrant eucalyptus. "This could be an addition to our lineup of bridal bouquets."

Imogen beamed. "I was thinking exactly the same thing. Wrote down the combination and sketched the arrangement in the book." She tapped her blue leather notebook with pride.

"I'll do the delivery," I said, suddenly thinking about how to kill two birds with one stone. "You go on home."

She looked delighted, but still paused. "Are you sure? It's my turn to lock up this evening."

"Absolutely. Don't think I've forgotten that you have a second date this evening. That's a big deal."

Her standards were, let's just say, so high that not many of the men she met got a second chance at impressing her.

"This one's nice. He's a pediatrician." She looked unsure.

"Okay, what's wrong with him?" I asked.

"Nothing. I'm wondering if he's too nice?"

"You are terrible," I said. "Give him a chance. I'm sure he'll get grumpy if you date him long enough."

She got her things together, and I told her I wanted a full report in the morning. I began the close-down, beginning with printing out the till's reports. While I waited, I opened a tub of Normie's favorite dried pineapple treats and fed him with the closest I've felt to love for that naughty bird.

"Not that I'm condoning bad behavior," I said, handing over another sugary cube, "but you did good today, Normie. That man needs to understand that not everything can be bought round here. Willowers have a lot of respect for the part of the world they live in, and most of us revere history."

"You know who might be able to help?" Norman said, his voice turning sly.

I looked at him.

"Our good friend Alex. He's back, you know. I saw him driving through the village as I flew over to Dennis's place."

So, I guess this is where I tell you about Alex. A little while ago, I helped Alex spruce up his ancestral castle and entertain a very discerning French vintner that Alex needed to impress. It had been a beautiful evening, and Alex had won the client. In return, he'd wanted to take me out for dinner to say thank you, but had been called to a supplier in Italy to finish closing a contract there. He would have returned to Willow Waters yesterday and, between you and me, I was excited to see him again and take him up on his offer of dinner.

You see, there were certain feelings stirring between Alex and me. Feelings that were tangible but complicated. Apart from the fact that Alex was generally reclusive—and his full title was Lord Fitzlupin, and he lived in a bona fide castle—he was also a werewolf. I know, right, how complicated can it get? But he still didn't know I was a witch. How we were going to proceed was anyone's guess. But that didn't stop me from wanting to find out.

I took out my broom and began to sweep the stray leaves and stems from the floor. I liked closing the store, going through each step, which signaled the end of another day. I found it soothing. More so when I put music on. I set my playlist to random and put in my earbuds.

I was busy sweeping and bopping away to Aretha Franklin when I heard my name. I turned and there was Alex. To say I flushed is an understatement. I was rivaling Dennis on the red cheek front. I quickly found my phone and turned off the music.

"Sorry!" I said. "I thought I'd locked the door."

Alex looked pleased to see me. That, or he was trying not to laugh at me. "Thankfully, you forgot. You've got quite the moves, Ms. Bellefleur."

I would have put my head in my hands, but I was too busy taking in Alex. He'd caught the sun while he'd been away, and the golden color further intensified the blue of his eyes. Even his jet-black hair seemed lighter, kissed by the sun. He was in his usual indigo jeans but had switched out the crisp button-down shirt for a luxuriously soft-looking cashmere jumper (that's a sweater in Britspeak). The result was relaxed and still *very* handsome.

It was time for a quick change of subject. "How was Italy?"

"Lovely, though tiring. Lots of work dinners, which I must say I find a bit grueling. All that small talk isn't really me."

"Must be terribly taxing, eating all that truffle tagliolini and cacio e pepe," I teased.

Alex laughed good-naturedly. "Lucky for you, it gave me some ideas about our dinner plans. That is, if you're still willing to accept my offer of dinner."

"Well, now you're speaking my language."

"Good," he said, and took a few steps toward me. "Do you trust me?" Although his eyes were still lively, there was something more serious in his tone.

Despite myself, my heart began to beat faster—in part because, without thinking, I knew my answer. "Yes," I said quietly.

"Good, then I'll leave the restaurant a surprise."

I usually didn't go in for surprises. Being a witch and all, I liked to know what was coming at all times and to be prepared. But I couldn't deny the sense that I was safe in Alex's hands.

"I was hoping you might be free tomorrow?"

"Well..." I said, stringing it out, "it's short notice, but... you're in luck."

Alex smiled. "It's a date. And now that's sorted, tell me—what's all the news in Willow Waters?"

No doubt he thought he was joking as Willow Waters was

normally a quiet village, but I filled him in on the return of the ex-Willower Dennis Ratslaff and his grand property purchase. Then I asked if he remembered Dennis.

From his expression, I could tell Alex did remember, and it wasn't a fond memory. He shook his head. "I can't believe he's come back to town."

"A view shared by many others."

"I was traveling around a lot back then, growing the business, so I never really knew him, except by reputation. He's a shifty character. Unless he's improved."

"From what I witnessed, he's worse than ever." I told Alex about Dennis nearly killing poor old Milton.

Any thought of violence against a dog was obviously upsetting to Alex. He made a sound like a snarl. "He'd better watch himself."

It occurred to me that if Dennis wasn't careful, he'd be getting a visit from a wolf.

"And that's not all." I explained about visiting Barnham House and his intention to rip out the historic gardens to make way for a pool, then I quickly described the ill-fated visit from Arthur Higginsbottom. "I betrayed Dennis Ratslaff's confidences, but some secrets shouldn't be kept. Even so, Arthur was unsure if they'd be able to act fast enough to stop him."

"We can't let that happen," Alex said firmly. He himself came from a long line of Willowers and had the utmost respect for history and the natural world, too. "Why don't I shift and go sniff around?"

I felt my eyes open wider. I was surprised to hear Alex referring to his canine nature so nonchalantly. But after seeing how Dennis had threatened the non-existent pigeons,

I wasn't too keen on Alex sniffing around as a wolf. I had a sudden image of that dreadful Aboriginal spear arrangement and shivered.

"I don't want you to put yourself in any danger," I said.

Just then Normie, who'd finished gobbling up all his treats, swooped down and landed on my counter.

"I'm better than a drone, doll face," he drawled to Alex, not me, which elicited another rumbling laugh. "I'll keep an eye on Barnham House, see what's going on, and report back."

CHAPTER 6

*E*arly evening on a June day in Willow Waters brought balmy weather and a golden light which lent the high street a dream-like quality. A few people milled along the stores, browsing if they were tourists or popping in for a last-minute gift or food item or bouquet if they were local. There was the faint smell of roasting garlic floating from the Italian restaurant, which tantalized my nose and made me think about my dinner. I loaded Gillian's flowers in my Range Rover and sent Norman to Café Roberto to let Char know we were ready to leave. She'd have to contend with a little detour on the way home, but I figured Char wouldn't mind swinging by Gillian's grand house.

Although I was being nice to Imogen by letting her leave early and doing Gillian's delivery myself, my reasons were a little selfish, too. My curiosity about *Gilly* and *Denny's* relationship was getting the better of me, although I suspected, too, that my witchy instincts were firing up for a reason.

Char waved from across the road.

I opened the Rover's door, and she and Norman slipped in.

"I hear we're taking a road trip," Char said.

She looked tired but content, and I smiled because that's exactly how it should be after a day's hard work. And trust Norman to call a delivery a road trip.

I nodded yes. "I wonder if Owen will be working," I said, as nonchalantly as I could muster.

Char and Owen Jones, Gillian's extremely hot gardener, had been hitting it off lately. The two were a great match. But neither of them was forthcoming about it, much to my chagrin. They talked cars, tattoos, and music—and acted like friends, but they had a spark so electric that it needed its own hazard warning.

Owen was older than Char, and he calmed her post-teenage angst without cramping her style. He'd been helping me at the farmhouse and had green fingers like I'd never seen. He got my struggling plot of peonies to finally bloom, brought off-cuts of surplus hollyhocks which far surpassed my own, and had even helped to lay a gorgeous stone path across the lawn. A keeper, right?

I enjoyed Owen's company, his straight-talking no-nonsense approach to everything from fertilizer to carbure-tors to being framed for a crime he didn't commit. Owen was solid, unflappable, and a good influence on the often-unruly Char. He'd been extremely loyal to the late Mr. Fairfax and stayed on to help his widow, even though the two had their ups and downs. I appreciated that quality of loyalty more than anything else.

Char was wearing drainpipe jeans, knees poking through giant holes, and a white T-shirt with a band's logo in silver that I wasn't cool enough to recognize. Her pink-tipped hair was pulled back in a messy high bun, and silver earrings in the shape of coiled serpents hung from her ears. As I put the car into gear, I noticed how she smoothed the strands of her bun and adjusted her T-shirt.

"Lemmington House is awfully big for one person," Char said. "I wonder if Gillian Fairfax will move."

"Or marry again," I said, thinking how much she seemed to like having a man around.

"That dame doesn't want to settle down," Norman opined.

I didn't tell him off for his inappropriate language. It was pointless. That parrot was not woke.

"It's enormous, considering that only one person lives there," I said. "But Gillian loves that house, and I can't blame her."

Lemmington House was one of the most beautiful and historic properties in the area. It was Grade II listed, built sometime in the seventeenth century, and had gorgeous semicircular bay windows under a thatched and stone roof. Touring the property was like walking around the set of a period drama.

"The Fairfaxes have lived in the Cotswolds for centuries as landowning gentry," I said. "Alistair's family was responsible for part of the more recent restoration of the water mill."

"Spare me the history lesson," Char replied, though not unkindly. "You sound like the nuns, except they were talking about old churches, which is even more boring."

"Ooh burn," Normie said in the voice of an American teen.

We passed The Water Mill—one of England's oldest inns —and then the gorgeous fourteenth-century church—over which Justine, the new vicar, presided—before I was forced to switch gears as we drove up the steep hill which overlooked the village.

Char fell silent, and when I glanced over at her, she looked a little wistful. She *had* been burned by her ex, Mick, who'd been in trouble with the law and gone on the run. Although she wouldn't admit it, I sensed that he'd knocked her confidence when he'd broken things off. Had enough time passed that she was open to a new romance?

I suspected that both she and Owen wanted to take things slowly. This was a small community, which made things super awkward if they didn't work out. And that made my thoughts turn to my own friendship that seemed to be warming up.

The lord of our local manor had definitely shown some interest in me. I liked Alex a lot, but also worried about what would happen if our incipient romance didn't work out. I'd made my home here in Willow Waters and wanted to stay, while his family had been here for centuries. If it came to one of us needing to leave the area, it was pretty clear which of us it would be. Not that I could imagine that happening, but I was still wary. We both had secrets, too, which made a normal relationship impossible.

Could it work?

I was mulling this point when I turned off the road and drove along Gillian's driveway, admiring the intricate topiary which framed both sides. Up ahead, I could see two figures outside Lemmington House.

As we got closer, I saw that it was Gillian and Owen. She was standing over him as he knelt and dug in one of the borders, which led to the grand doorway at the front of the house where Gillian's Mystic Blue BMW was parked. Owen was wearing his gardening uniform of green overalls and looked a little wary. I knew that Gillian was mostly a hands-off boss, but she was also a woman of particular tastes. She'd made it clear that she'd like him to do more for her than trim her hedges, and he'd turned her down. Was she trying again?

I parked on the gravel drive. And even from this distance, I was pretty sure Owen was happy to have his chat with his boss interrupted.

"Do you want to come with me?" I asked Char.

But the sight of Owen had made Char suddenly shy, and she shook her head.

I got out and waved to them both. Gillian was a tall, very attractive former model in her forties. She was dressed in a deep-burgundy silk dress which tied in an elegant bow at the waist. Her blonde hair was pulled back in a sleek chignon, allowing her dainty silver hoop earrings to glint in the sun. The woman simply didn't do casual.

I hefted the large bouquet out of my car and walked over. I was dying to know what she'd think of Dennis Ratslaff's offering.

She leaned over Owen and peered down at the soil. "What do you think, Peony?" Gillian asked as I grew closer. "I was suggesting that the lavender would look better if it was raised in the bed a little."

Owen's head was bent over a clump of new lavender, so Gillian couldn't see his eye roll. Had they really been discussing the garden?

Essentially a shy man, Owen was uncomfortable navigating his role as village heartthrob. With his rugged good looks, messy crop of brown hair, and broad smile which transformed his face, Owen had had his fair share of female attention in Willow Waters.

Gillian had tried to seduce him while her husband was still alive, and Owen had turned her down in no uncertain terms. She'd tried to have him fired, but after her husband died, to my surprise and probably Owen's, she kept him on. Perhaps she felt bad for her earlier treatment of him. Maybe he was a link with her late husband. Or maybe she planned to try to seduce him again. Who could tell?

"It's your call, Mrs. Fairfax," he said in his warm Yorkshire accent. "We could build it up a little, no problem."

Hah. They might work together every day, but he kept his distance from her by calling her Mrs. Fairfax and making it clear they belonged in different social worlds. He obviously didn't want to play the Lady Chatterley's Lover game.

"Maybe just a little," she said.

He nodded at me as I came closer. There was a slight sweat on his brow, and he put down his trowel to wipe it away. "That's a beauty of a bouquet." He stood and brushed some soil from his knees.

"Goodness," Gillian said, finally paying attention to me. "Are those for me? How pretty."

"They sure are," I said, handing her the flowers.

She took them and reached for the card. "From Leon? How sweet."

Who was Leon? I could not keep up with Gillian and her intrigues.

"Not Leon," I said.

"But whoever could they be from?" She lowered her voice. "I'm not exactly Mrs. Popular in the village."

Ouch. Well, I couldn't really argue her point, so I stayed

diplomatically silent and then gestured to the card. I wanted to see her expression as she read *Denny's* message with his crude reference to *recent events*.

Do you think that's cruel of me? I hope not. It's just with Gillian, it's hard to gauge an honest reaction. She was so finishing-school calm and collected that she was able to conceal even the deepest sense of shock, shame, or surprise. If you could bottle Gillian's stiff upper lip, then you could make a pretty penny.

Gillian read the card. I watched closely as her eyes widened and her brow furrowed almost—but not quite—imperceptibly. The result was a little startled. But in a good way? Bad way? I couldn't be sure.

She looked up at me, her eyes narrow and shrewd again, her forehead impossibly smooth. "Dennis Ratslaff is here? In Willow Waters?" Then she glanced behind me as though he might be there. Was that paranoia? Excitement?

I replied that yes, Dennis had returned. I had met him this morning, and he'd bought a home in the village. I held back from explaining that Dennis had already made a pretty dire impression on quite a few of us this morning, including me.

Now Gillian's shock was evident. She had visibly paled, and she scratched at the nape of her neck distractedly. "Dennis Ratslaff bought a home here in Willow Waters? Are you certain?"

It wasn't like I'd invent a story about a man I didn't know existed until a few hours ago, but I couldn't exactly say so to Gillian. "I'm certain. He said he bought Barnham House." I could resist adding, "Off the Internet, if he's to be believed."

Owen whistled through his teeth. "I dunno who this guy

is, but he's one lucky fella to score that place. The gardens are some of the best I've seen in this part of the country." He didn't say more, but I wondered if he was thinking of applying to be the gardener there. It would get him away from Gillian, and he'd be working in a garden that was famous.

Gillian must have been truly in shock because she didn't even flinch at the prospect of losing her favorite gardener. "Barnham House," she repeated, her voice softening and turning coy. "Dennis must be doing very well." And then, almost to herself, she said, "He just arrived in town and immediately sent me flowers." The color was returning to her face now, and her light eyes brightened further. "Well, well."

I was starting to feel uneasy. Was Gillian so easily flattered by an expensive bouquet? Surely she'd received hundreds in her lifetime. These were special, but not I'm-going-to-overlook-my-past-heartbreak special. And what about the Leon she'd mentioned?

"How did he look?" she asked.

I'd never seen him before, so couldn't say he'd aged well or anything. I stuck with something I knew would interest the status-conscious Gillian. "He was tanned like he'd been on a long vacation. And he arrived in a red Lamborghini Aventador Coupe."

A slight widening of the eyes again. "He's done *very* well for himself, then." She pushed a curl over her ear with a well-manicured hand. "Perhaps I'll pop by and welcome him to the neighborhood."

After all that I'd heard about Dennis's murky past in Willow Waters and the hints that he'd left Gillian broken-hearted, I was surprised at how quickly Gillian was seduced by the idea of his return. She already had a beautiful home and the kind of lifestyle most people could only dream about. What did she need Dennis for?

"Well, you know where he is," I said, trying not to sound too dismissive.

"Yes. It's unfortunate timing, as I've just started seeing someone. And he's rather possessive."

Now it was my turn to try not to look surprised. I knew Gillian was fond of men, but she'd only been widowed a month. A month was nothing.

"Don't worry, Peony," she said, smiling. "It's not serious. Just someone to have a drink and a meal with occasionally. You must understand how lonely one can get. And this new one's so different from my dear Alistair, who was such an old-fashioned gentleman. Leon is a real macho man. I'm enjoying how possessive he is, how protective."

Personally, that sounded like my worst nightmare. But who was I to judge? Gillian was speaking to me like a confidant, and in many ways, she had my sympathy. We couldn't have been more different from one another, but I did know what it was like to lose a husband and to feel like an outsider in this village. So I felt a strange kinship to this woman, and I wanted to intervene, warn her that there was something off with Dennis.

But would I be telling Gillian anything she didn't already know? He'd left the village with a trail of destruction behind him. Then he'd broken Gillian's heart, or so he said. It took guts to come back here. Or did it? Maybe it wasn't guts. Surely you would have to be bordering on the sociopathic to retire in the village where you'd ruined lives and disgraced yourself? Couldn't Gillian see all this for herself? Or was she truly blinded by the spoils of his riches?

I opened my mouth to say some of what I was thinking, but then closed it again. We weren't friendly enough for me to insert myself into her personal life. Instead, I could keep an eye on things from afar and get involved only if it was strictly necessary. Plus, I had Norman as my spy. If Gillian was in any danger, I'd soon know about it.

She patted her chignon. "But there's nothing wrong with welcoming an old friend to the neighborhood, is there?"

Owen and I caught each other's eye. I had a feeling that we both smelled trouble.

CHAPTER 7

The silent moment of communication between Owen and me was broken by the sound of a rumbling engine. Dread flooded my stomach and made it turn. Could it be? Would he? Surely not.

I swiveled, expecting to see the now unpleasantly familiar sight of a red Lamborghini zooming up the driveway. But thankfully, there was no need to brace myself against another encounter with Dennis Ratslaff. The car was a Mercedes. It was silver, sleek, and expensive-looking but not showy. Much more in keeping with an average Willower's style. I breathed out.

Suddenly, I felt the bouquet being slammed back at me.

"Take it," Gillian demanded. "That's him now. My new beau. I can't have him thinking that these are for me—I'd never hear the end of it. Say you made a mistake in the address or something."

I looked over at Owen, stunned, but he simply shrugged and returned to his lavender. Talk about awkward. I didn't know what to do with myself.

The silver Mercedes parked beside my old Range Rover, and a beefy man emerged. He was dressed in tight black jeans and a short-sleeved black T-shirt that looked as though it was a size too small. No doubt the fit was on purpose: his arm muscles were enormous, chest and shoulders the broadest part of his body. Personally, I found the overall effect a little like a walking triangle. But, hey, each to his own. This guy obviously spent a lot of time in the gym, and he wanted people to know it.

As he came closer, Gillian began to melt. Not literally, of course, but her entire body language shifted, and she became softer, almost gooey.

"Darling," she purred.

"Honey," he replied in a voice much higher than I'd anticipated. Then the man pulled Gillian in for a hard kiss.

I was already uncomfortable. Now I felt embarrassed and wished I was a million miles away from here.

His dark hair was shaved close to his head. He had the most unusual amber-colored eyes, which were framed with thick black lashes. He had a square jaw covered in a stubbly black beard.

I stood rooted to the spot until Gillian finally gave a girlish laugh and pulled away. I took the opportunity to remove Dennis's note and stuffed it into my pocket.

Side by side, the two of them made for an odd-looking couple. Everything about Gillian was so polished and feminine. This man looked like he lived in sweaty gym clothes.

And then, as he noticed me and my enormous bouquet, his expression darkened.

Without introducing himself, the man came toward me, frowning. I clutched the bouquet tighter, but refused to be intimidated. It would take more than some muscles and a frown to unsettle Peony Bellefleur, thank you very much.

"Who's sending you flowers, then, Gill?" he asked, still staring at me. It was pretty rude. I mean, he hadn't even introduced himself, and here he was eyeballing me.

Gillian looked panicked, but I wasn't going to pretend I got the wrong address like she'd asked. In a small village? Who'd believe it?

"I'm Peony," I said, extending my free hand. "Owner of Bewitching Blooms on the high street."

"Leon Barker," he replied, shaking my hand. The gesture was reluctant and yet its execution bone-crushing.

I winced.

"And like I said, who's sending Gill flowers if it's not me?"

Gillian looked at me with naked appeal.

What could I do? "The flowers are for Owen," I said.

Owen's head snapped up. He'd escaped the situation by getting back to work, tenderly patting more soil around the newly re-planted lavender bush. He cleared his throat, stood, and then nonchalantly accepted the extremely romantic bouquet of white flowers as if it was an everyday occurrence.

"You getting married, mate?" Leon cracked. "You'll make quite the blushing bride."

But Owen just shrugged and said thank you. As if he cared what this beefcake thought.

"Not bridal flowers," I replied, trying to defend Owen without embarrassing him further. "Thank you flowers. From me. Owen's been helping me with my garden." I gave Leon a significant look. "Fresh flowers brighten any home. Even a bachelor's. In fact, *especially* a bachelor's."

He shrugged his enormous shoulders. "Not the sort of thing we go in for, in my line of work."

"Which is?" I asked as politely as I could muster.

"I have a shipbuilding company in Estonia."

"Leon's being modest," Gillian cooed in a voice thick with admiration. "He owns one of the biggest shipping companies in Estonia." Then she turned to Mr. Muscle. "Come inside, darling. It's lovely to see you. I wasn't expecting you."

They said their goodbyes and went into the house. As Gillian closed the front door, she mouthed a silent 'thank you.'

I felt suddenly and uncomfortably complicit in her romantic drama.

I turned to Owen, who'd caught sight of Char. He waved, but the girl still didn't get out of the car. Argh, what was wrong with her? It was also weird that Normie had stayed put. Were those two finally on the same page about something?

"So, there's a new man on the scene," I said, gesturing over at the house while stating the obvious.

"She met him at a party," he said gruffly. "The bloke lives in Chipping Norton, but he's been coming around quite a bit already."

I could tell from Owen's tone that he was not a fan. I wasn't very impressed with Leon Barker, either. Although at least he drove more carefully than Dennis.

"It was a good idea to give me the flowers," Owen said. "I'll keep them in water and give them to Gillian when he's gone."

I knew I should just leave Owen to his work, but honestly, I was worried about Gillian. As you know, I'm not her biggest fan, but I empathize with her situation. Being widowed in Willow Waters, I mean, not juggling men. And, right now, it seemed like she was in the middle of two men with big egos. I smelled danger.

I said as much to Owen, who listened thoughtfully as I explained my run-in with Dennis earlier. His jaw dropped open when I told him about Vera and Milton—no one had a softer spot in the village for dogs than Owen. Well, maybe Alex, but that was for personal reasons.

I held back about the planned digging of the historic gardens at Barnham House. I knew it would anger Owen, and I didn't want him to rush in hot-headed. Arthur Higginsbottom was on the case. And if he needed backup, we'd be there.

"I don't know what it is about Gillian," Owen said, "but she loves to invite trouble."

"I'm glad she has you around," I said, "to keep an eye out."

Owen said he'd do his best, and I got back in my car. At least I'd delivered the flowers to the right address, if not the right person.

I hit the accelerator and divulged Gillian's potential love triangle to Char. But she just rolled her eyes and asked what we were having for dinner.

BACK AT THE FARMHOUSE, dinner was already underway. Jessie Rae and Hilary were being unusually cooperative in the kitchen and cooking up a storm with some new farm produce Hilary had picked up on her way home from the university. Hilary was a retired lawyer, happily divorced without children. She was studying for a master's degree in Classics, and her head was always in a book. Lucky for us, sometimes that was a cookbook and this evening she was making a wild mushroom risotto.

Before we'd even got through the kitchen door, Hilary recruited Char to scrub the mushrooms with a toothbrush. I was given a grater and a block of cheese from the local dairy. My mom was opening the wine—her favorite job. The talk was of Dennis Ratslaff. As I said earlier, Willow Waters was a small village with little inclination for change. Someone like Dennis turning up here, almost running a dog over, and buying one of its most gorgeous houses was a big news day.

"I just don't understand how anyone could treat Vera that way," Hilary was saying. "She's a lovely person, and she adores that dog. I cannot imagine saying something upsetting to her." She pushed diced onions around the pan, prodding at them with a spatula as if she were prodding Dennis in the chest.

"She's well-loved, that's true," Jessie Rae said as the cork popped from the bottle of white wine. She handed it to Hilary, who tipped the Arborio rice into the pan and added a nice glug of wine for good measure.

"Literally everyone has been talking about him in Roberto's," Char said. "Like, it was nonstop."

"Do people remember him?" I asked.

"Some do," she said, "and those who weren't here then or were too young got filled in pretty quick. No one had a good word to say about Dennis Ratslaff. It was all bad-mouthing."

"Really?" Hilary asked, turning away from the pan to stare at Char in surprise. "I heard some women talking in the greengrocer, and they seemed pleased to have a rich, single man in town."

Char rolled her eyes. "Well, those who remember him hold a grudge. They're not happy to have a shady trouble-maker back."

Hilary nodded. Without speaking, Char tipped the sliced mushrooms into Hilary's pan. Hilary looked up, surprised, and then smiled.

Char had known exactly when Hilary needed those mushrooms. It was part of her witch's instinct growing, but I wondered if Char even realized what forces were guiding her half the time. I'd decided to go easy on Char—it had taken so long for her to even accept she was a witch, but after experiencing her first witches' coven last month, she hadn't progressed much in her craft—bar spontaneously igniting a few candles. Maybe it was time to push her a little harder. Something else to add to my to-do list.

Hilary stirred the risotto thoughtfully as my mom poured us all a glass of wine.

"They've been talking in my store, too, lassie," Jessie Rae said before taking a deep drink. "The spirits, that is," she added quickly.

Hilary sent me an amused look.

"Och, yes," my mom continued, her silver bangles clicking as she waved her hands. "They were stirred up today. I believe he's brought in swirling clouds. I predict a storm ahead."

Today I was inclined to agree with my mom's predictions.

Finished with the cheese, I joined Char at the round kitchen table.

"In other news," she said, "I've got a side hustle going on."

"Side hustle?" Hilary asked. "Is that a new kind of dance?"

Char threw her head back and laughed, exposing her one front tooth, which crossed in front of the other. Her serpent earrings jangled, and she explained that her side hustle was a way to make extra money on the side of your day job. "One of my regular coffee store customers was talking to me about his banged-up truck and asked how I'd managed to fix Frodo. He'd noticed it on the roads. So, I told him I'm a bit of a gear-head, you know, and then he wanted me to try to fix his. Cash job, like. So, I'm going there tomorrow evening to give it a go."

"That's great, Char," I said, feeling pretty proud of my protégé. She was a brilliant mechanic. Working on cars was adding to her life in the village.

She grinned. "More money for the move to London."

Hmm. Was Char still really set on moving to the Big Smoke? I thought we'd done a good job of showing her the delights of our pretty little village. Besides, I was enjoying having her around. Maybe more than I let on.

At that moment, Norman flew in from the garden. He'd obviously been eavesdropping as he landed on Char's shoulder and said, "Give it a break, Cookie. You love it here."

Char laughed. "Yeah, maybe I like it here more than I thought. But it's not exactly bright lights and fast cars."

I sighed. "Well, with Dennis Ratslaff and Leon Barker around, you can't say there aren't fast cars here."

Char grimaced. "The Lamborghini is special for sure, but I wouldn't choose one. Too flashy. Bet he doesn't even know how to use half its features."

Jessie Rae was busy pouring herself more wine. She flopped onto the seat next to Char. "I think we're all missing a trick here," she said mysteriously.

"What's that, Mama?" Norman asked.

Jessie Rae tutted. "I've asked you not to call me that."

Norman ignored her.

"The real gossip is my little lassie's date tomorrow."

I spun to face my mom. How did she know that? Were her powers even stronger than I thought?

"Norman told me," she explained.

Norman cackled. "Couldn't keep that sweet nugget to myself."

"Wait, what?" Char asked, eyes wide. "You're going on a date? You've really been holding out on me. With who?"

"It's *with whom*," Hilary corrected. "And it's with Alex Stanford, of course." Hilary wasn't even a witch, and she'd immediately worked out what was going on. She turned to me. "Good for you, Peony. You'll be the envy of the whole village."

Despite myself, I could feel my cheeks reddening. "It's not a date, but a dinner to say thank you for helping him out with the castle and his client."

"Yeah, right," Char said bluntly. "Willow Waters' most elusive and eligible bachelor is taking you out to say 'thank you' for pretending to be his wife."

"His partner, not wife," I corrected, and then just as soon as the words escaped my mouth, I realized how silly they sounded.

Normie started to make kissy noises, and the women laughed.

"Enough!" I said, though really I couldn't help but smile. "You guys are worse than high-school girls."

"But where's he taking you?" Hilary demanded,

completely ignoring my desire to drop the subject. "It's got to be somewhere fancy."

"What will you wear?" my mom asked. She reached over and touched my arm. "No denim."

I stared down at my denim shirtdress. "Thanks a bunch, Mom."

"Another little black dress," Hilary suggested. "Like last time. Or maybe you should be more casual." She paused. "Do you have time to go shopping?"

"I like you with your hair up," Char commented distractedly. She'd opened a car magazine and was leafing through its pages.

"Yes, definitely up," my mom said. "She has lovely ears, doesn't she?"

"Save me," I murmured.

Hilary laughed and said we should probably think about eating.

I was about to thank her when my mom suddenly stood up, sending her chair clattering.

"What is it?" Char asked, looking startled. "Is something wrong?"

Jessie Rae began to sway.

"Mom?" I was accustomed to Jessie Rae and her strange episodes, but no one else was.

"They're back," she replied in a faraway voice. "The dogs. Why are you surrounded by dogs?"

I took the bottle of wine from the table and topped up my glass. It was going to be tricky keeping Alex's secret from my mom.

"And there are puppies. I always thought of you as a cat person."

These dogs were appearing to her more and more often, though I hadn't a clue what the puppies were about. Could I lie and say I was thinking of getting another pet? But no, my mom wouldn't buy that for a second.

At that moment my familiar, Blue, softly padded into the kitchen, stopped, stretched out her marmalade legs, then raised her pretty face.

I scooped her up and let her snuggle on my lap. "Nice timing," I whispered into her fur.

"Puppies!" my mom repeated shrilly. "I always thought of you as a cat person."

"Exactly," I replied, holding Blue tight as proof. "I *am* a cat person."

CHAPTER 8

*T*he next morning, Imogen and I were super busy making our way through the orders. Friday was a bustling day in Willow Waters, full of expectations of the weekend to come. We felt it in the village more than others might, as so many people had second homes in the surrounding areas and flooded in from London and other cities on Friday afternoons. It boosted that childhood feeling of the weekends as sacred. And personally, I loved it.

Imogen had enjoyed her date with the pediatrician, but decided that there was no spark. We both agreed that without chemistry, a relationship probably wasn't worth pursuing. Still, she wasn't upset. No doubt she'd have another date lined up soon.

So, the store was full and customers were in a good mood. Okay, okay, I'll admit that I was in a good mood, too, and it was more than just a Friday feeling. You might have already guessed that it was because I was looking forward to having dinner with Alex.

Could I call it a date? I wasn't sure. However, I definitely felt that elusive chemistry with Alex. All morning my mind had been running riot with scenes from my first night at Fitzlupin Castle. I thought of how natural it'd felt to pretend to be his partner for that night. What a charming host he'd been to his new client. How sweet and earnest he'd looked in the kitchen, cooking with the confidence of one of those TV chefs. And I mean one of the sexy ones.

And then I recalled how we'd said goodbye at the end of the evening. How he'd draped the pashmina round my shoulders, fastening it with Char's brooch. I remembered the scent of him, fresh and woodsy, when he'd bent closer to me and kissed both my cheeks, French style. He'd lingered for a moment. And as my heart raced, I'd closed my eyes, certain that he was going to kiss me, but he'd pulled away as the sound of my ride home had rumbled in the drive.

"Um, Peony, hello?"

It was Imogen, laughing. "Where did you just go? You looked like a daydreaming schoolgirl."

I blushed. She'd hit the nail on the head. A daydreaming schoolgirl was the perfect description of me. I'd allowed myself to go all gooey. Over a man. Honestly!

"Sorry. I didn't get enough sleep last night," I said. "I'm a bit dozy."

"Really?" Imogen said with a coy smile. "I thought you were looking well-rested today. Your eyes are so bright. And you have rosy cheeks. Or is it just a new blusher? I heard Dior's new one is great." She flicked her glossy hair over one shoulder and then neatly tied a bow around one of the ready-to-go bouquets she was making.

Now I really was blushing. "It's the shirt," I said, gesturing to my outfit. I was wearing a new magenta broderie anglaise shirt with cut-off jeans, and I did genuinely think it perked up my complexion.

"Well, let's see what this gentleman thinks of it," she said, pointing at the door. "A handsome man is on his way in."

Normie let out a sharp wolf whistle—thankfully before the door opened and Neil, Vera's grandson, walked in. Then Normie said, "I'm off to Barnham House for another snoop about."

I was glad he was on the case. It was crunch time to halt Dennis's plans to dig up the historical gardens to put in a swimming pool. I hoped Arthur Higginsbottom could do something to stop him. Norman disappeared over the top of Neil's head and glided into the street.

In jeans and a white shirt, Neil looked much more casual than when we met yesterday—but just as stressed. He ran a hand through his salt-and-pepper hair and came straight to the counter and said hello.

"Morning, Neil," I said. "How are Vera and Milton doing after the shock of yesterday?"

"Not so good. That's why I'm here. I'd like to get some flowers for my grandmother. I'm worried about her." He softened. "The bouquet you made for Rosie was so pretty, I thought I'd get her something for herself."

As happy as I always was to get more business, the exchange made me even more mad at Dennis. That man had only been in town twenty-four hours, and yet he'd already stirred up so much trouble. Vera and Milton shouldn't have been subjected to his road rage.

"Is Vera still in shock?" I asked. "Dennis Ratslaff gave us all a terrible fright. It must be much worse for Vera." I thought about how I'd feel if someone driving recklessly came close to harming Blue, and my blood began to boil.

Neil shook his head. "It's not so much shock as it is fear. She's refusing to take Milton farther than her garden. She's so worried that Dennis will try to harm her dog."

Oh no. Poor Vera. That was no way to live. And old or not, Milton still needed his exercise.

Imogen shook her head. "That Dennis is a brute," she said. "My parents remembered him, and they didn't have a single good word to say."

"Seems like that's most people's opinion round here," Neil agreed. "I was just in Roberto's and people are still talking about Dennis's past in the village. The words *chancer*, *swindler*, and *dangerous* kept coming up. But I'm not going to let him frighten my grandmother." He clenched his fists, unclenched them, and then clenched them again.

He went on to explain that he'd bought a box of her favorite truffles from the deli and also wanted to bring home flowers to brighten Vera's mood. Once she was smiling again, he'd swoop in and suggest they all go for a walk. "And if we see Dennis out and about, then I'll make it very clear that I will fight to protect my family." As he spoke, Neil's right hand formed a fist.

Imogen caught my eye. She looked alarmed.

I was surprised by how quickly Neil had angered as he talked about Dennis, but I understood the innate desire to protect his family. "I think flowers will be just the trick to get Vera feeling herself again. Did you have anything in mind?"

Neil shook his head and confessed he didn't know much about flowers.

"That's what we're here for," Imogen said, flashing her

winning smile. "And luckily, we know your grandmother well. Vera has traditional tastes but nothing fussy. Would you like me to put something together for you?"

I watched with pleasure as Imogen showed Neil around our selection of blooms, picking out some of the stems which would complement the bouquet Vera had bought from us just yesterday and that we knew she didn't grow in her own garden.

Imogen was the perfect assistant. She knew the locals better than I did. I doubt I could have told Neil which flowers Vera grew in her garden! Imogen knew exactly when and how to switch on the charm. It also helped that Neil was undeniably handsome. Sadly for Imogen, he was very much taken.

"How long are you and your family staying with us?" I asked as Imogen began clipping the selected blooms.

"We're here for more than a holiday." He explained that with the arrival of the baby, he and his wife had been talking more about what kind of future they wanted as a young family. "Life in London is great with fantastic restaurants, galleries, and museums, but the fast pace is wearing us out. Plus, the cost of property is astronomical. We want to try a slower style of life."

I couldn't imagine attempting to raise a family in London.

He said they needed more space for his daughter and the new baby, which hopefully included a garden. "We're in a top-floor flat at the moment, and there's not much room. And since I mostly work from home these days, we were thinking about moving. It would be nice to be closer to Gran."

Imogen was nodding as she deftly made up a pretty bouquet. "I know exactly what you mean," she said. "I studied in London and spent a couple of years there afterward, but I missed the village too much. Nature over petrol fumes any day." She held up the bouquet. "What do you think?"

"Perfect," Neil said. "These will make my grandmother so happy."

I rang up the bouquet, and Neil paid with a fancy platinum credit card. He thanked us again, and I asked him to pass on our regards to Vera and Milton.

As he left, I turned to Imogen to say good job, but before I could get the praise out, Normie came crashing back into the shop. He was flapping and squawking.

"What's going on?" I asked.

"Come quick, Peony. There's trouble at Barnham, trouble at Barnham!"

I looked at Imogen.

"Go," she said. "I've got the store covered. Don't let that brute get away with anything else."

I grabbed my bag and rushed out into the street with Normie. Just as I was about to slide into my Range Rover, I spotted my mom wandering toward me, looking mystical.

"Mom?" I said, throwing my bag into my car. "What is it?"

Jessie Rae shook her bangled wrists. They chimed and clinked, and she swayed to the sound. "A sacred resting place has been disturbed."

Oh man. I didn't want to be dismissive of my mom, but I really didn't have time for this. "Get in the car," I commanded.

Norman said, "Go, go, go."

My mom got into the Rover in a semi-trance, and then we were off.

"Ohhhh, the spirits are unsettled," my mom warbled. "They have woken. They are blinking."

"Step on it, Cookie," Normie added.

Sometimes my mom's conversations with spirits were random. Other times they were clues to our world. Annoyingly, I never knew which one it was at any given time. But both she and the talking parrot were making me anxious to get to Barnham House and see what was going on.

The sun was beating down hard by this point, and I rolled down the windows and let the wind rush into my Range Rover. I was going to need a cool head for whatever scene I was about to walk into. I took deep breaths and tried to block out my mom's strange moans. They were making me as unsettled as the spirits were making her.

We arrived at Barnham House. I quickly parked in the front and leapt out with Normie and my mom in tow.

"Follow me," Norman said, and flapping and squeaking, he led us around the back of the enormous house, which—as you can imagine—was quite the entrance.

I could hear raised voices over a rumble of machinery.

Uh-oh.

As we turned the corner of the house, there was Arthur Higginsbottom standing on a path and shouting. Dennis was a couple of feet away.

"You can't excavate your garden!" Arthur yelled.

I was surprised to see Arthur had completely lost his temper. Yesterday, he was so mild-mannered—I didn't think he had it in him. But this was what Dennis did to people in the village. First with peaceful Vera, who swung her walking stick at his car, then with her grandson, Neil, rolling his fists just at the mention of Dennis's name.

"This is a historic property," Arthur added. "It's listed."

But Dennis didn't appear bothered in the least. He was

wearing red shorts and a white polo shirt and the nastiest expression of distaste I'd seen in a long time. He took a step toward Arthur and loomed threateningly over the smaller man. "I can do what I like," he boomed. "And I will!"

Arthur stared at him for a moment, aghast, and then broke into a run. He was heading for the wildflower meadow, which Dennis was set on swapping for a swimming pool. Looking enraged, Dennis followed him, and so did we.

I gasped as the gardens came into view. An enormous digger was already tearing up the perfectly manicured green lawns. We were too late to keep the lawns intact, but I was determined that the destruction would stop there.

At the sight of us (which must have been pretty wild—two sweating women, two angry men, and a parrot) the digger stopped and the terrible sound of its engine died out. Dennis screamed at the operator to keep digging. But no cigar. He climbed down from the cab. He was wearing a black baseball cap, which he removed when his feet hit the grass.

"Get back to work!" Dennis shouted again.

But the operator was shaking his head. He could only have been twenty years old, and as he came toward us, there was a look of pure shock on his tanned face.

Of course, Dennis was far too enraged to adjust his tone and spat, "What's wrong with you?"

Again, the young man shook his head, this time so vehemently it was as if he were shaking out water after being thrown into a pool. The likes of which we were here to stop from materializing.

Finally, nervously bending the peak of his baseball cap back and forth, he said, "I've found bones, sir. I can't keep going."

CHAPTER 9

"*B*ones?" Dennis yelled at the digger operator. "What the hell do I care about bones? So a previous owner buried their pet dog in my back garden. Boohoo. The fewer mutts around here, the better."

"No," the young man said. "It's not dog bones. It's—"

Dennis cut him off. "Don't be so ridiculous. Do the work I'm paying you for."

I heard my mom's moans as she wandered over to the hole beside the digger. "Oh, the spirits aren't happy. They are unsettled. You've desecrated a sacred place."

"Who's this old witch?" Dennis shouted.

"Don't speak to my mom like that," I snapped back.

He glanced around until his gaze locked on me. He did not look happy. "Get her out of here."

I rushed over to the hole where my mom was still swaying. Arthur Higginsbottom was right behind me.

I joined my mom and slipped an arm around her slim waist. I peered down, following her gaze. In a short space of time, the digger had managed to wreak a lot of havoc. The void in the earth was about twelve feet wide and six deep. It was dark in there, the soil reddish in places and crumbly.

I squinted harder. "What is that?" I whispered.

Buried within the mounds of soil was something creamy white. It was protruding from the earth at an angle. I shuddered. It looked like an arm, and I was desperate for someone to contradict me.

Arthur coughed but didn't offer an answer. Suddenly, everyone was silent. My mom, Normie, even Dennis Ratslaff, which was a real first.

And then the sound of a car engine broke the reverie.

"What are you doing here?" Dennis shouted from behind me, breaking his short silence. "Are they selling tickets out front?"

I turned and was filled with relief when I spotted Alex. I was convinced he'd know what to do. "Alex," I called. "Over here."

As soon as he saw me, he broke into a sprint and raced toward me, his gait light and nimble, despite his build. Another situation and I might have taken pleasure in watching him run, but at that moment I was simply too confused to take it all in.

"Am I too late?" he asked when he reached my side.

"No," I said quietly, and explained that work had just begun, but then stopped because the digger had uncovered bones.

Alex peered down. But then the sound of the digger started up again. We all turned at the same time.

I couldn't believe what I was seeing.

"What on earth?" Arthur muttered.

Dennis had clambered into the cab of the digger. He

was sweating, swearing, and trying to figure out how to make the thing work. The gears ground and clashed terribly.

"Oh, have mercy," my mom groaned. "The spirits are raging."

"They're not the only ones," I said.

"Don't just stand there, stop him," Arthur demanded of the young digger operator, who was watching the whole scene with his mouth wide open.

"Right. He can't drive the digger. He doesn't have the authority." The young man struggled to hoist himself up the digger's steps, but then the machine lurched forward.

"Sir, I must ask you to stop!" he called out as he fell back onto the grass.

"This has gone far enough," Alex said firmly.

I looked at him and something passed between us. "No," I murmured.

But it was too late.

Alex jumped into the enormous hole. The digger was lurching its way back to the edge of the hole.

"Get out of there!" Dennis roared, still driving the digger toward Alex. "Or I'll dig you out myself."

But Alex paid no heed. He scrabbled around in the soil, digging with impressive zeal. I won't say he was burrowing like a dog at the beach. Let's just say he was digging down quickly.

I closed my eyes and took my mom's hand. Silently, I summoned my powers to make the digger stop in its tracks. My mom squeezed my fingers tight. But I needed to say a spell, and I needed my mom's power, too.

I felt our joint power, and Norman's claws wrapped

around my shoulder as though the parrot knew I needed him, too. I whispered,

"Spirits of the North, South, East, and West
The sacred earth is suffering unrest
This digger must stop, that is for the best
So I will, so mote it be."

I was so rattled, I wasn't sure that I'd had the proper focus, but there was sudden silence as the digger stalled. Dennis swore loudly and tried to turn its engine over again, but it spluttered and shook.

My eyes flashed opened and there was Alex, looking back up at me.

He was holding a human skull.

FOR A MOMENT, everyone froze around the hole. It was as if we'd agreed to all stand still in order to let the image of the skull sink in.

Each of us reacted differently. My mom began to murmur something which sounded Latin. Arthur inhaled and exhaled so loudly it crossed my mind that he might be close to hyperventilating. Dennis thumped his fists against the steering wheel of the digger with a thud, thud, thud. Alex stared at the skull in wonder.

It was all very Hamlet.

For my part, I was aware of the sun beating down on the nape of my neck, the sound of birds, and the light breeze which ruffled through the garden's many green and luscious leaves. I had tuned out of the moment and only came back to the problem at hand when Dennis climbed down from the digger.

He stomped over and went to the opposite side of the dreadful hole which he'd caused. He stared down as we all focused on him. As I'm sure you'll already be imagining—he was furious.

"What is this place?" he yelled. "That's a human skull. What imbecile got himself buried here?"

I turned to Arthur, whose moment had clearly arrived.

He looked shaken, but there was also a spark in his eyes. "It could be ancient," he whispered.

Wow. I hadn't thought of that. Now not only were the grounds of protected historical interest, they were also of archaeological interest.

The head of the local historical society was visibly thrilled at the secrets of the past we were about to uncover. "This reminds me of when Richard III was discovered," he said, watching Alex continue to turn the skull in his hand and examine it from every angle.

"Richard III?" I asked, feeling confused. "Was he found in someone's backyard?"

"No, dear. Under a car park. In Leicester."

I had no idea what the relevance was, but clearly Arthur was excited.

But I couldn't admire the new find. I was too confused. Normally, my witch's instinct would have alerted me to a nearby death. I should have felt the heaviness of someone passing, like a weight in my own body. But I'd felt nothing— just the desire to protect the gardens. Was something off with my powers? Had the digger even stopped because of our magic? Or had Dennis managed it all by himself? I wanted to ask my mom for help, but I couldn't, not in front of the others. I was going to have to trust myself.

I turned to my mom, who was now suspiciously silent.

Jessie Rae's eyes were closed, and she was swaying on the spot, her long, curly red hair flowing down her back.

I put a hand on her arm. "Mom?"

Her green eyes flicked open. "The sacred place has been desecrated," she repeated, a terrible sadness in her voice.

We all watched as Alex gently laid the skull back on the earth.

"Right, that's it!" Dennis yelled. "Everyone get out of here. You can all clear off. This is my property, you hear me? So get off of it!" His face had maintained a livid redness I'd never thought possible for a human being to sustain so long without keeling over. He pulled out his phone. "I'm calling my lawyer."

"I'm calling my boss," the digger operator said.

And then firmly and loudly, Arthur said, "And I'm calling the police. *And* the university archaeology department." He stepped toward Dennis until he was less than a hand's-breadth from the man's red face. "Mr. Ratslaff," he said, in a voice so calm it was chilling, "if that digger so much as moves an inch, there will be trouble so deep not even your ill-earned cash will be able to buy you out."

Dennis's jaw dropped. And I'll confess mine did, too. Where had the mild-mannered history nerd of yesterday gone? The intensity of the discovery had transformed Arthur, had imbued him with a boldness no one, I bet least of all Arthur, could have imagined.

I turned to my mom, stunned. But she wasn't paying

attention to the altercation between the two men. She was still staring at the skull.

"Could I have a little help getting out?" Alex called up.

A small smile flickered at my lips. It was easy jumping into an enormous hole to save the day, but much harder to get out.

Automatically, Jessie Rae and I went to its edge, linked one of our hands in the other's, and then held the remaining ones out to Alex.

Alex looked perplexed, clearly not wanting to offend us, but also unsure of our ability to actually get him out of there.

"We're much stronger than we look," I said. "Trust us."

I closed my eyes and concentrated my powers on channeling a greater strength into my mom's hands and mine. I felt a ripple of electricity go through me and breathed a sigh of relief. My powers hadn't completely abandoned me.

Alex gripped each hand and then gently and slowly walked up the side of the hole. "Thank you, ladies," he said when he stood on firm ground again. He was sweating at the temples, and there was soil on his shirt and under his fingernails.

"That was quite the move," I said, laughing a little, "leaping into the hole like that in front of moving machinery."

"Very brave," Jessie Rae said admiringly. "The spirits cherish your actions. They don't want any more disturbances."

Alex looked at me. I knew that he was honorable and wanted the digging to stop just as much as any of us, but I also knew part of the reason he'd jumped was instinct. He'd seen the bones and leapt with the canine desire to dig them up.

How many times had I seen a Willow Waters dog on the green or in the meadows playing with a bone? They loved to chew and received a pleasing rush of endorphins as they did so. Surely a werewolf had some of the same instinct. Not that I was questioning Alex's bravery, but I could tell he'd enjoyed himself down there.

"What, or who, do you think that is?" I asked. I mean, digging up human skulls in the garden wasn't an everyday occurrence where I came from.

"I've no idea," he said, "But Arthur's right. It could be a very old grave. Between the police and the university, they'll have the best people to research who that was."

He glanced over at Dennis, who was making a show of calling someone on his phone. "I don't trust that man. I'm going to call my lawyer, too," he said. "The more official records of this find, the better." He dusted himself down as if he needed to present himself properly to make the call. Then he did what no one else had thought to do. He took out his phone and snapped some photos.

Only now did it occur to me that Dennis might dispose of the human bones and pretend they'd never existed. His word against ours. The photographs made that impossible.

"I'll escort you two off the property," Alex said, still eyeing Dennis with hostility. "I don't want you alone with that maniac."

I thought he had a good point. "Dare we leave him?" I asked, wondering if I should be brave and refuse to leave until the police arrived, but Alex assured me that Arthur

Higginsbottom wouldn't vacate the premises until he was certain the find was in safe hands.

Certainly, Arthur was standing by the open hole with his arms crossed over his chest, giving off an aura that pretty much said, *Just try to throw me out.*

"Okay," I said, and Mom and I walked with Alex back around the house to the front where we'd parked—and where his dark-green Jaguar now sat beside my Range Rover. I couldn't fathom how he'd arrived at exactly the moment the bones were uncovered. "Were you planning to visit Dennis?" I asked Alex. "Welcome him to the neighborhood?"

He shook his head, looking amused at my suggestion. "I was driving by, and I sensed you needed me."

And he was definitely the first man who'd ever said those words to me. Including my late husband.

Our gazes connected. I understood that he'd felt my need with an animal instinct and shivered slightly.

"Thanks," I said.

He waited while we got into my car: me, Mom, and Norman. Then, with a wave, he got into his own vehicle.

I didn't pull out right away. I needed a moment.

Mom said, "Alex Stanford is a lovely young man. But he's got a very peculiar aura. He's not a witch, is he, dear?"

I kept my smile hidden. Trust a mother to want to know everything about the man her daughter was dating. Or *thinking about* dating, I reminded myself.

"I don't think so," was all I said.

In the back seat, Norman made a noise like a muffled parrot guffaw.

I needed to draw her attention away from Alex. Plus, I was puzzled. So I asked, "Why couldn't I sense that someone had passed there? Normally, I feel the heaviness of death, but I didn't get that. What's going on?"

Immediately Jessie Rae went into soothing mom mode. "Ooh, lassie, there's nothing wrong with your powers, if that's what you're worried about. Whoever is buried there, it's not a recent death. The burial site remained undisturbed for a very long time. You wouldn't have been able to sense anything. Too much time has passed."

I was overcome with affection for my mom. Yes, her rantings and communing with the spirits often occurred at inopportune moments, but her connection with the earth and with people was so special. Jessie Rae was unique. I was lucky she was my mom.

"Thanks, Mom."

Arthur came around to the front of the house. I was certain he wouldn't have left the dug-up bones without strong provocation so I decided to wait. We might not be the greatest backup, but we had some skills, Mom and I.

A red-faced Dennis came stomping around, following Arthur Higginsbottom. When he saw my car still parked, he went a deep shade of purple. "I told you all to get off my property."

"Not until the police arrive," I said firmly through the open window.

"And the university archaeology team," Arthur added, looking very relieved to see me and Mom. He came close to my Range Rover, and I had a crazy picture of him jumping in and us roaring off, Dennis chasing us all the way. "The police are on their way," he added, sounding impressed.

I hoped it was true. I didn't like the look of Dennis in a rage.

The digger operator came toward us more slowly. He scratched his head, bemused at the morning's drama. "It's like being on one of them TV programs where they discover some old king in the ground," he said to Arthur. "Or Viking treasure."

"Or Viking treasure, indeed," Arthur replied, his voice quivering with excitement.

CHAPTER 10

*A*fter the arrival of the police, lawyers, university staff, and the young digger's manager, the rest of us had left Barnham House and returned to our respective days—a little worse for wear and worn out, but also full of excitement. In truth, I'd have loved to stay. It really was exciting being present when a possible historical relic was uncovered, but I also had a flower shop to run.

The rest of the afternoon passed (thankfully) without drama, and I was determined to put the events of the morning out of mind and concentrate on my work.

As I prepared bouquets, took orders, and prepared for the busy Saturday trade, I looked forward to a lovely evening with Alex. He was picking me up at seven. I felt a clutch of excitement when I imagined a real date. He had his secrets, and I had mine, but I also felt we had a lot in common.

Imogen insisted that I go home early. She would lock up, which I appreciated very much. "But I want all the details tomorrow," she added as I was leaving.

I GLANCED AT THE CLOCK, aware that time was ticking and Alex would be here soon. The atmosphere at the farmhouse was like a sorority. If I'd thought the women in my life had been excited when I'd had dinner with Alex and his client at the castle, it was nothing compared to the fever pitch reached as I prepared for a proper dinner date with Alex.

To my surprise, the worst offender was Hilary, who was happily divorced and had sworn off men entirely. She wasn't even interested in a little mild flirting, let alone dating. But for some reason, she'd been especially excited by the idea of Alex taking me out. I was sure it wasn't a case of living vicariously. I mean, Hilary's idea of a great night was ordering in a spicy curry and re-reading *The Iliad*. But as I put the finishing touches to my outfit, she kept popping her head around the door.

"Goodness," I said, as she stepped into my bedroom for the third time. "Do you not trust me to get dressed alone?"

Hilary laughed. Blue was at her feet. My familiar padded across the wooden floorboards to circle my bare ankles. I'd just stepped into my new dress, and Hilary was appraising the final look. To my relief, she was still smiling.

"Now that's nice," she said. "New?"

I nodded. On the way home from work, I'd mentally run through my wardrobe and dismissed everything I owned. Nothing seemed right for an evening with Alex. And although I liked surprises, it didn't help that I had no clue where we were going. Knowing Alex, I guessed he'd choose a restaurant that would be smart but understated. I had plenty of clothes suitable for greeting customers and hauling bouquets of flowers, but I really didn't have a dating wardrobe.

Char had picked up on my mood and suggested a fashion pit-stop. There was a small boutique, near The Mermaid Pub on the other side of the village, which I'd always considered too upscale for my needs. But Char insisted that we look, then practically bullied me into spending some hard-earned cash. I'd tried on several simple but beautifully cut summer dresses. The cornflower blue had caught my eye immediately. Made from brushed silk, it had thin straps and flowed to my ankles in a flattering bias cut. Smart, understated, perfect.

Hilary was still appraising me, and I began to flush. I'd kept things sleek: a bun at the nape of my neck and a pair of small silver hoops, the metal hammered so as to reflect the light.

"Good, good," she murmured.

I felt like a mare in a horse show and told her so. "You look like you're about to recite my stats," I added, only half joking. "Strength, speed, stamina."

"Mating potential," Hilary teased, and then chortled.

Blue meowed as if in agreement.

"Don't you sell me out, too," I chided.

But Blue just jumped onto my bedspread, rolled nonchalantly onto her side, and purred.

I shrugged and then slipped on a pair of silver sandals, which I'd rooted out from the back of my wardrobe.

Again, Hilary nodded approvingly.

I took a look in the mirror and was pleased with my efforts. I had several flower perfumes which I wore on rotation. I surveyed the glass bottles, trying to pick a scent which would please but not overpower Alex's keen sense of smell. I settled on one which showcased the gorgeous aroma of heliotrope. The fragrance blended the signature bloom with a hazy veil of gardenia and magnolia with simmering Sambac jasmine.

As I sprayed my pulse points, I couldn't help asking Hilary why she was so interested in my evening with Alex. "Not that I don't appreciate the thought, it's just that it's not like you," I said, carefully watching her face in the mirror.

"You're right," she said, meeting my eye. "I don't care for idle gossip or romance." She paused and then in a softer voice said, "But I do care about you."

I turned to face her. The evening light was golden, and it picked out the auburn strands in her hair.

"Hilary," I began, but she cut me off.

"Don't think I'm getting soft," she said, "but remember that I moved in here just after Jeremy died. I've watched you put your life back together, Peony. I've watched your business grow. And this is the last piece of the puzzle. I've seen the way Alex looks at you. And how you respond to his look." She put her hands on her hips. "Frankly, it's heartwarming."

While she spoke, I felt my eyes getting wet. A lot had changed over the last three years, but Hilary had been there —a quiet, dependable housemate who had soon become a firm friend. I stepped toward her, but knowing that she'd hate a hug, grasped both her hands in mine instead and squeezed.

At that moment, the doorbell sounded.

Hilary checked her watch. "And he's punctual. I can't bear a tardy man."

I laughed, maybe a little too hard. I was as nervous as you'd expect. This was my first dinner alone with a man in... Well, years. Would I even remember how to make polite dinner conversation? At least we had today's exciting find to talk about. Maybe it wasn't everyone's idea of first-date conversation, but I thought skulls and bones could get us through the appetizers at least, maybe all the way to the main course.

"What are you waiting for?" Hilary asked, handing me my purse. "Your carriage awaits."

Downstairs, I was mortified to find my mom and Char had already opened the front door. I rushed over, determined to save Alex from their line of questioning.

"But you *will* get her home before she turns into a pumpkin at midnight, won't you?" my mom asked with an arch glance at my date.

"Jessie Rae," I said, "that's quite enough. And it's the carriage which turns into a pumpkin at midnight, not Cinderella. Get it right."

I swept past her and Char, bidding them both a pleasant evening, and ushered Alex out, promptly shutting the door behind us.

Alex, to his credit, was laughing good-naturedly. "Those two are quite the—"

"I don't even want to know what they said to you before I came down," I said. "Spare me the embarrassment."

"Well, perhaps I can embarrass you in a more pleasant way by telling you how beautiful you look this evening."

I happily accepted the compliment and for the first time looked at Alex properly. He was wearing a navy suit and a crisp white shirt with the collar unbuttoned at his neck, exposing a few dark chest hairs.

"And you look quite fetching yourself," I replied, determined not to blush.

He thanked me and told me that he'd given George the night off. "I thought it would be more...normal for me to drive us, rather than relying on George."

George was Alex's butler, although Alex hated calling him that. George had worked for the Fitzlupin family estate all his life, as had his father before him. I was fond of George, but I agreed that it was nicer to be alone with Alex.

We walked to where his Jaguar was parked, and he opened the door.

I slipped onto the leather seat and settled myself.

Alex got in and as he started up the engine, he sniffed, once, twice, and then said, "Gardenia with heliotrope? Maybe a little jasmine, too?"

I grinned. "Nailed it. I hope it's not too overpowering?"

Alex shook his head. "Like a tropical summer garden in bloom."

We pulled out of the driveway, and I realized I still had no idea where we were going.

Reading my mind, Alex said, "I booked the trattoria in Kingham. It's a bit of a drive, but the food is incredible. Giovanni, the owner, is passionate about wine, and we import some rare bottles from Sicily for his cellar."

I told him it sounded perfect. Italian was one of my favorite cuisines, and after the day we'd had, I was famished.

As we drove, the sun sank toward the horizon, its yellow-gold tones turning orange. It was a balmy evening, and the Jag's windows were down. The wind ruffled Alex's dark hair as he chatted about his recent work trip to Italy. He'd been in Umbria and described a restaurant there which he'd love to take me to.

He didn't bring up Dennis or the bones, so I left the

subject alone, too. Maybe he was saving that subject for when we were sitting down facing each other, reaching for conversation. Or maybe he simply thought there were better things to talk about than horrible neighbors and death.

He looked more relaxed than I'd ever seen him, and I wondered if that had to do with my knowing his deep-held secret. Had it freed him in some way? For the first time, I contemplated what it would feel like to tell Alex about my being a witch. Would I feel free? Or like I was betraying myself and my coven?

"I don't know about you, but I'm famished after the drama of this morning," Alex said.

I murmured my agreement, then decided I couldn't stand not knowing what was going on at Barnham House. "Do you know what happened after the archaeological team arrived?"

"I had a quick call with Arthur Higginsbottom, but all he could tell me was that the garden had been sealed off and Dennis Ratslaff was in trouble with, well, pretty much everybody. Thank goodness you got there when you did. Who knows what further damage that man could have inflicted on a sensitive find?"

"Arthur got there first," I reminded him. "But I was glad to be there for backup, and really happy when you turned up."

"Why were you there?" he asked.

Why hadn't I prepared a story? Of course, he'd wonder how I happened to be at Barnham House on a work day with no flowers in hand to indicate a delivery. I couldn't tell him a parrot had told me to go there, but luckily my mom had been with me and everyone knew Jessie Rae was subject to strange visions. "Mom felt a disturbance in the spirits," I said, keeping my voice light.

"She was correct, as it turned out." He glanced at me. "Did you inherit her gift?"

He didn't sound as though he were asking whether crazy ran in my family, more as though he respected my mom's sight. I respected her gift as well, though I didn't share it.

I could just tell him now that I was a witch and be done with it. But again, I hesitated. Once the truth was spoken, I couldn't take it back. I wasn't ready to share something so intimate with Alex, especially as I had coven sisters in the area who might not appreciate me blabbing.

"No," I said at last. "I'm no medium." After a short pause, I said, "I'm glad Dennis is officially in trouble with the historical society and the police."

That man had been a menace from the moment he sped into Willow Waters. But now wasn't the time to get riled up. I was determined to switch off and enjoy the evening.

Before long, we arrived in Kingham, and Alex slowed as we tried to find a parking spot—a perennial problem for all the prettiest Cotswold villages. Kingham was a hilltop market town and was once the site of an Iron Age fort, though nowadays the center of town was filled with galleries and a treasure trove of antique stores. It was more upscale than Willow Waters, and I was glad of my new dress.

The outside of Giovanni's trattoria was unassuming, just a dark canopy and simple monochrome sign, but inside revealed an elegant Milanese lounge-style space complete with graphic parquet floors, smoky mirrors, and retro backlit walls. I looked around, taking it all in, feeling a bit like Cinderella, after all.

The maître d' greeted Alex as an old friend and kissed both my cheeks when Alex introduced me. "I've kept the best table in the house for you, sir," he said in a lyrical Italian accent, "but perhaps you would like an *aperitivo* in the garden first?"

Alex glanced at me, and I nodded. The maître d' guided us through the restaurant to a set of French doors which opened out to a spectacular terrace, surrounded by herbaceous bushes twinkling with lights. The man pulled out my chair and asked what I'd like to drink. I asked for a Campari spritz, ready to throw myself whole-heartedly into the feeling of an Italian holiday.

But as a waiter brought us the tall glasses filled with the sparkling drink and slices of orange, a loud, angry voice shattered the peaceful scene.

"I'd like to sell *him* a car," a man's gruff voice said, all but shouting the words.

Alex and I turned at the same time toward the voice. A man—who'd obviously had a few too many—was scowling at a woman who was trying to shush him, clearly embarrassed. He was a stranger to me. Middle-aged and gone a bit to seed, with the mottled cheeks and watery-eyed look of a heavy drinker.

"Who is that?" I whispered.

"That's Ralph Dawson," Alex replied somberly.

I knew that name. "Isn't he the guy who bought one of Dennis Ratslaff's cars and crashed into the front of his house when the brakes failed?"

"The very same," Alex said. "I guess he's heard that Dennis Ratslaff is back in town."

"Ratslaff is thumbing his nose at me. It's an insult." Ralph Dawson's voice was creeping up a notch. His loud complaints slurred.

His girlfriend, or wife, said, "It was a long time ago. Why don't we forget him and enjoy our evening?"

Ralph shook his head. "Can't enjoy anything with that man back in town. Well, I let him get away once. I won't do it again."

"Please, Ralph," his companion said, glancing around. "You're making a scene."

"*Making a scene!* Who are you? My nanny?"

The woman gave up trying to shush him and asked a waiter for the bill. It arrived more promptly than one might expect and, with Ralph still throwing out insults, the couple left.

I watched them go, relieved when the peace of the terrace was restored. I felt sorry for anyone who'd been harmed by Dennis Ratslaff, but tonight I wanted to think about something else.

I pictured the bad energy sweeping out of the door as though a broom had pushed it. That done, I settled down to enjoy my date.

"Now, where were we?" Alex said, obviously sharing my thought.

CHAPTER 11

I shook off the image of Ralph Dawson's belligerence and fixed my attention once again on the wonderful restaurant and the attractive man sitting opposite me.

I sipped my drink, enjoying the bittersweet taste of the Campari.

And right then I realized I'd had no need to worry about being on a date again. Not with Alex. He was a man I felt I could trust. And, since I'd kept his secret identity to myself, he must know he could trust me, too.

Alex took the lead and asked me thoughtful questions about my mom, my housemates, and what it'd been like growing up in Maine. And I did my best to answer just as thoughtfully. It had been a long time since someone had taken an interest in me this way, and I'd almost forgotten what it was like to really show myself to someone, to allow them an insight into who I was.

Alex listened, but every time I asked him something in return, he'd answer briefly and turn the conversation back to me. I'd thought that knowing his deepest secret might encourage him to open up further. I was wrong. But I wasn't going to push it. Alex would speak more freely when he felt comfortable.

The maître d' soon reappeared and led us back through the French doors to a banquette table at the rear of the restaurant. It was partially hidden by a red partition wall but open enough to watch the room.

The maître d' pulled out a velvet chair for me and then Alex, then hesitated with the menus. "I don't mean to be presumptuous, sir, but I don't expect you'll require the wine list. Or the menu, in fact, as we both know the chef's tasting menu is the only sensible option. If the beautiful lady has an appetite, that is." He stopped and looked at me enquiringly.

"Of course." I would love a tasting option.

"Very well, that is settled," he said.

Alex ordered a bottle of red wine, the name of which meant nothing to me.

Dinner began with a light vegetable broth and a sumptuous *giro* antipasto, followed by an intense tomato bruschetta and amberjack brushed with an olive, caper, and anchovy pesto. We both ate heartily, and Alex visibly relaxed.

After regaling him with some choice anecdotes about growing up with Jessie Rae (imagine what career day looked like when my mom came to speak to my elementary school class about her job as a medium), finally I was able to steer the conversation round to Alex's childhood. I wanted to know what it was like for him growing up in that enormous castle. I knew nothing about his parents, for example, or where he'd gone to school or whether he'd wanted to go into the family business or it had simply been expected.

He smiled his perfect smile at my eager questions and spoke slowly, deliberately, weighing his words as if he knew what power they held over me. He told me that his mother had died when he was three years old. He had no real memories of her, but he could still recall her scent. Her death had been quick—a pulmonary embolism that had gone undetected and suddenly taken her from them. His father never got over the loss and threw himself into the business, traveling more frequently and for longer stretches of time.

"That's why I'm so close with George," he said. "The man practically brought me up."

My heart went out to Alex. Like him, I'd never really known my father. He was a tree surgeon and had died before I was even born. Although Jessie Rae communed with him regularly (or so she said), I'd never felt like he was part of my life, despite knowing that he was watching over me.

We chatted comfortably as dish after sumptuous dish appeared.

I was about to bite into delicious grape-stuffed sardines from Puglia when a laugh bellowed through the dining room. I stiffened, recognizing that grating guffaw. "Oh no," I murmured. "Please don't let that be who I think it is."

But, of course, my fabulous first date was rudely interrupted by the appearance of Dennis Ratslaff—and Gillian Fairfax. Worse, they were being seated at a nearby table. Dennis was so busy telling a story that he didn't notice us, and Gillian had all of her attention on her dinner companion.

I didn't need to point out the new arrivals to Alex.

He glanced at them, then back at me, looking exasperated. "I booked this restaurant specifically because I thought we'd have some privacy."

My heart fluttered at the word *privacy*. I liked that he'd wanted me all to himself. I suspected that Dennis had made the same calculation. Or maybe Gillian had suggested this place. She'd be wary about being seen in Willow Waters if her new man, Leon Barker, was as controlling as he'd appeared.

I smiled at Alex. "Let's just ignore them. Gillian's questionable taste in men is really none of our business."

He nodded, but Dennis couldn't help but draw attention to himself by acting the big shot. Every word that came out of that man's mouth was a hundred decibels louder than anyone else. Gillian's flirty tittering was also impossible to ignore. She was attracting a lot of attention herself in a slinky silver dress, her blonde hair wound into a classic chignon, and her lips painted ruby-red. She looked like a movie star, and Dennis was loving every minute of it.

In his booming voice, he asked the waiter for a bottle of wine, attempting very badly to pronounce its name in French. Then he gave up. "You know the one, mate. It's the most expensive bottle on the menu. Me and the lady are celebrating," he announced.

I heard the waiter respectfully say he would bring it immediately.

Alex snorted.

"What is it?" I asked.

"The most expensive wine in Giovanni's cellar is a historic relic rather than a drinkable wine. He only keeps it on the list so they can charge two thousand pounds for a bottle of wine."

I felt my eyes open wide. "Two thousand pounds for one bottle?"

Since fine wines were his business, my shock seemed to offend Alex.

"A lot goes in to growing wine," he said, "and the best vintages sell out, so to preserve a few bottles for fifty years or more without them turning to vinegar is a real art."

I raised my eyebrows and tried to channel Gillian Fairfax. "So why aren't we drinking two thousand pound wine? Aren't I worth it?" I was joking, of course. Mostly. I'd never, ever seen a snobbish side to Alex before, and it tickled me that he had one.

He leaned over and took my hand. A tiny thrill ran up my arm.

"You are worth more than a wine that's too old to be enjoyable. It's valuable because it's rare, not because it's good, and a true connoisseur would know that."

I held Alex's gaze, my heart in my throat as he looked back with his sparkling gray-blue eyes.

We both went back to our food, but I knew I'd remember that moment for a long time—if not forever.

I also knew the moment when Dennis Ratslaff glanced over and recognized me and Alex. I could feel his gaze, hard and heavy with arrogance. Then he said something to Gillian. And I felt her, too, glance over at us. I kept my eyes on my plate, pretending that I hadn't seen them. All of my previous run-ins with Dennis didn't make me inclined for small talk with the man. And, as for Gillian, I wouldn't know what to say to her. No doubt she felt the same, as she didn't call out a greeting.

I heard her hushed voice questioning Dennis. From the

gruff way he leaned in and lowered his voice, I suspected he was giving her his version of events earlier that day. I suspected the story he was telling Gillian would bear little resemblance to the truth.

The fun leaked out of our evening having those two seated near us. I was using a lot of energy trying not to acknowledge their presence or eavesdrop on their conversation. We stopped swapping confidences, Alex and I, on the chance that they might try to eavesdrop on us as well.

Fortunately, the last course, dessert, was all that was left. I was so full and agitated that I doubted I could do it justice.

However, I was determined to give it my best shot. We'd been promised a pear and ricotta cake that sounded amazing. I was debating the wisdom of coffee when I received yet another shock.

Leon Barker had walked into the trattoria. And by the way he was advancing on Gillian, it wasn't a coincidence. He swaggered toward her table chest first. Like yesterday, he was wearing tight black jeans and a short-sleeved black T-shirt. The glare on his face was fierce.

He stood out in this sleek and sophisticated restaurant. His presence was so strong, other heads were turning. I watched, aghast, as his fists clenched and unclenched, and then clenched again.

"That's Leon Barker," I whispered to Alex. "Gillian's new beau."

"He doesn't look happy," Alex replied.

"And he's Possessive with a capital P. This is going to be ugly."

At that moment, Gillian sensed eyes on her and looked up and across the room. She froze as she saw who was striding toward her table. Dennis was busy talking, pausing only to take large swigs of wine. It was like watching a car crash about to happen, each person moving in slow motion, coming together in an unavoidable, catastrophic collision.

Biceps and triceps on full display, Leon announced himself with a high-pitched, yet terrifying demand. "What is going on here?" His amber eyes flashed.

Dennis slouched back in his chair and stared at Leon, bemused. "'Scuse me, mate? You lost or somethin'?"

"Dennis Ratslaff," Gillian said, trying to sound like a society hostess, "meet Leon Barker. Dennis is an old friend of mine, Leon." Her voice was soft and placating, but it didn't soften Leon's anger. If anything, his fury grew.

"You said you were going to the pictures tonight, Gill. Why did you lie about that if this is nothing but a dinner with an *old friend?*"

"I changed my plans at the last minute," she said, sounding as feeble as her excuse.

Leon snorted. "And dolled yourself up for this fat twit."

Dennis abruptly stood. A fork clattered to the floor. "Now just a minute, there. You watch your mouth," he said in his loud voice.

By now, the two men had the attention of the entire restaurant. The maître d' disappeared behind a curtain and returned with a man in a suit who I assumed was the manager.

Gillian's face was pink with embarrassment. She glanced at me, as if I might save her, but what could I do?

Leon stuck out his square jaw, thrusting his stubbly black beard toward Dennis. "You keep your grubby hands off my girlfriend. *Mate.*"

"*Your* girlfriend?" Dennis snorted and crossed his arms, rejecting Leon's declaration. "This is *my* Gilly."

"She's playing you for a fool," Leon retorted.

"*No one* calls me a fool." He stepped out from behind the table and squared himself up to Leon.

But Leon towered head and shoulders above him, and this appeared to send Dennis over the edge. A spluttered tirade began, so vehement that I could only make out single words.

Rude.

Intrusive.

Mad.

Money.

The manager and maître d' were trying to smooth over the situation with hand gestures and calm words. I looked around. Not a single person was eating. The drama had transfixed the entire restaurant. Gillian appeared both humiliated and scared.

Beside me, Alex emitted a quiet snarl. I turned, surprised. Alex was watching the scene with his teeth slightly bared. I sensed he was losing control and wondered if anger could make him shift—maybe he was vulnerable at other times, not just the full moon.

The last thing this scene needed was a man metamorphosing into a wolf, so I said his name softly. "Alex."

I could tell his attention was being dragged to the conflict. I took both of his hands and held them tight. His skin was rough, the palms so large it was a struggle to contain them in mine. But I gripped them tightly and concentrated on generating a river of calm which could flow from my body to his.

"Breathe," I whispered, and modeled deep breaths in through my nose and out through my mouth.

Alex fixed his gaze on me, and with wonder, I watched the internal struggle in his gray-blue eyes. He was wrestling with his nature, determined not to let the anger win. And then something changed. His shoulders dropped, his eyes calmed, and he smiled at me.

"Thank you," he said quietly and then leapt to his feet.

I watched as Alex approached the quarreling men. The manager and maître d' were having no effect and retreated gratefully.

"Gentlemen, kindly take your disagreement outside," he said in a firm, commanding voice. His words broke the spell of their rage.

"Good idea," Dennis said and strode toward the French doors leading to the terrace.

With a single nod, Leon followed him, while Gillian remained frozen in her seat.

Elegant and unruffled, Alex turned to address Gillian. "Shall I call my driver to take you home?"

In that moment, my heart melted. He'd seen Gillian's embarrassment—and everyone still gaping at her—and wanted to make this easier for her.

"No, thank you," she replied, clearly mortified and close to tears.

"You're welcome to join us if you'd like," he added.

In a tiny voice she thanked him but said she'd call a taxi.

Alex motioned to the maître d' and made the request. The man hastily agreed, and Gillian followed him out of the dining room—in the opposite direction from where the two men had disappeared onto the terrace.

"That was kind of you," I said.

He waved my praise away.

"Alex," I began, and then faltered.

Was it okay for me to mention his shifting? Would he prefer me to pretend I hadn't noticed that near growl? If the shoe was on the other foot, I didn't think I'd want him talking to me about being a witch. I decided not to bring it up, but Alex saw my hesitation.

He leaned closer and said, "I nearly shifted. Thanks for stopping me."

"Does it happen like that sometimes?" I was pretty startled.

"For the most part, I've learned to control my emotions, so I'm not triggered into shifting, but those two got to me."

"Because they were both yelling at Gillian?" Did Alex have feelings for his old friend's widow? It wouldn't be surprising if he did: men seemed to lose all sense in the face of Gillian's beauty and poise.

But Alex looked shocked. "No. Because they were upsetting *you*."

I felt my eyes widen. During the whole scene, I thought I'd been attuned to Alex's emotions, but he'd also been tuned into mine. I *was* upset at the scene, and I suddenly realized it was because I was concerned for Gillian's safety. Somehow, she'd embroiled herself with two men who both had big, aggressive egos. For many reasons, I didn't trust Dennis as far as my powers could throw him. And I didn't trust a man like Leon, whose possessiveness made Gillian so worried she'd insisted I lie about her receiving a bouquet of flowers.

Voices buzzed and glasses clinked, and the returning sounds of pleasurable feasting reached my ears. The dining room had swung back to its usual rhythm. Our dessert arrived, and I decided to chance a coffee, hoping it would help me regain *my* rhythm but wouldn't keep me awake later.

"It must seem strange to you," Alex said, "to be with someone who could change into an animal before your eyes."

I had to stifle a sarcastic comment about frat boys and bad teenaged dates behaving like animals. Alex was being serious. And here was my opportunity to tell him that I was different, too.

But as a witch, I'd learned from an early age to be private, and not even my late husband knew much about my powers. I'd grown up knowing that I was different, you see, and that set me apart from the kids in my neighborhood. It had been a struggle to control my powers. I was always opening windows and doors without getting up from the sofa. One time I'd even accidentally set a vase of flowers on fire. I know, I know, not a good start in life for a future florist.

So I learned to hide away before I did anything in public that my mom wouldn't be able to cover up or laugh off.

Now that I knew Alex's secret, and we had openly acknowledged it this evening, I so badly wanted to tell Alex about all of this, but something held me back again. I needed to discuss my predicament with my sisters. And yet, could I tell the coven I wanted to share my secret with Alex without revealing his? It wasn't like I could betray his secret in order to share mine. It was so complicated. But the desire to be truthful was so strong that I decided there and then to call a coven meeting and ask my sisters' opinion.

And then I silently berated myself. Alex and I had gone for one dinner. And now I wanted to confess my deepest secret. I needed to slow this down. I didn't even know what *this* was.

Alex shared a quiet conversation with the maître d' and then our bill appeared. The manager came out again and thanked Alex profusely. What the heck? Wasn't it normal to pay for your dinner?

Then I had an epiphany. "You paid for Dennis and Gillian's dinner, too, didn't you?"

He looked a little abashed, as though I'd caught him out in some way. "I asked the maître d' if Dennis and Leon were still on the terrace. He told me they'd left. I couldn't let the restaurant get stuck with Dennis's unpaid bill. It wouldn't be fair."

And that was one more black mark I silently added to Dennis's tally. He'd ordered a two-thousand-pound bottle of wine and probably every expensive thing on the menu, and then he hadn't returned to pay his bill. It didn't matter what the circumstances were. He'd pulled a dine and dash.

Alex and I walked out into the street. The evening had cooled considerably, and I shivered in my new dress. Alex slipped his arm around me, and we crossed to his car in a silence which would have been relaxing if the sensation of his arm around me wasn't sending tingles through my whole body.

We stopped at his Jag, but just as Alex was about to open the passenger door, he turned to face me. Above us, the moon shone and illuminated the chiseled features of his face. The affection in his eyes quickened my heartbeat, and I could feel my chest rise and fall.

And then it was happening. His hand brushed my cheek, then cupped my face and tilted it toward him. I breathed in the scent of him and felt my body soften, melting beneath his touch and trusting that he would hold me and keep me upright. When his lips brushed mine, something clicked inside me. I opened my eyes, delighted. He pulled back, grinning.

I leaned into him and kissed him again, firmly, insistently, until I forgot where we were or even my own name—so intense was the sensation of his lips on mine.

CHAPTER 12

a car drove by and lit us up. We pulled apart—me with a nervous laugh. Alex opened the passenger door for me. I settled in. A few seconds later, Alex was beside me. We didn't speak as he started the car, but the atmosphere between us was charged with electricity.

We'd taken a big step forward.

I was sorry that the passing car had interrupted our kiss, and yet not sorry to take a breath and think about where we might be headed as a couple. The memory of Alex's lips made my own lips tingle. But our future wasn't without its problems.

I looked at Alex, but he was focused on the road ahead. Even after three or four wonderful hours together, I still couldn't guess what he was thinking. I wasn't even certain what I was thinking. There was this budding romance to savor, but I couldn't help worrying about Gillian and her messy love triangle. What had happened after the two men left the restaurant? Had they beaten each other to a pulp? Had one or both of them gone to Lemmington House to confront Gillian? With luck, someone—probably the restaurant manager—had called the police to report the brewing fight.

Or was I being overdramatic? Perhaps the men had simply gone home.

I gazed out the car window. The streets were empty, and the moonlight lit up rows of characterful stone houses, a few with warm yellow lights sneaking through the gaps in their curtained windows. I tried to imagine what those households were doing with their Friday night. A cozy film with popcorn on the couch? A dinner party for friends? A Scrabble championship? Whatever they were up to, it had to be more normal than my own life.

Sometimes I wished things were a little less complicated. Then again, I'd probably be bored without a chatty parrot and nosy witches in my farmhouse and a werewolf taking me to dinner.

As we left Kingham and headed toward Willow Waters, I wondered whether I should call Owen to warn him to keep an eye on Gillian and her two angry men, but I wasn't sure I should interfere. Gillian was capable of calling Owen or the police if she needed protecting. Still, I felt uneasy. She and I weren't close enough that I could call or message her to make sure all was well, but tomorrow I'd find an excuse to speak with her.

The road we were on would pass by Barnham House. The closer we got to Dennis Ratslaff's new home, the more my instincts began to twitch. In spite of a full belly and the happy feeling that romance was in the air, I felt as though Alex and I were driving into shadows.

Something in me was springing to attention as I sensed

danger. It was potent. A dark, heavy feeling pooled in my belly—like a lake of black ink.

What had my mom said earlier? *The spirits are unsettled.* I had the strange feeling that Dennis's destruction had awakened something terrible. A Pandora's box of revenge. But I couldn't tell where the feeling was coming from or for whom it was intended. All I knew was that sometimes the past needed to stay in the past. Buried.

"Do you sense something in the air?" I asked Alex.

He lifted his head and sniffed. Was that how he read the world? By scent?

He said, "Someone had a barbecue earlier this evening. And they burned the potatoes. But otherwise, everything appears to be normal. Why do you ask?"

I decided to share a bit of myself, at least. Even if he put it down to women's intuition, he might as well know that I was feeling more than a ripple of unease.

"I don't know," I said honestly. "Maybe I have a bit of my mom in me, but something's not right."

"Do you think Dennis Ratslaff and Leon Barker actually hurt each other? I'd assumed they were more bark than bite, but perhaps I should have taken their conflict more seriously and followed them out on the terrace." He glanced over. "But that would have meant leaving you."

I wasn't sure if he meant alone at the table, or alone with Gillian, or simply without him. Whichever it was, I was glad he'd stayed. Frankly, I'd have ended up following him, if only to make sure he remained human.

"I don't know if they'd hurt each other. Maybe. I'm worried about Gillian, too. They were both so possessive of her."

"Do you want to drive by Lemmington House and make sure she's safe?" he asked, as though it were a normal request.

"No." I told him I'd call her in the morning.

He nodded. "Perhaps, after dropping you off, I'll drive by Gillian's place on my way home and make certain all's quiet."

I liked this plan a lot and tried to think about my farmhouse and prepare an account of the evening for the nosy women who, I was pretty sure, were waiting up for me. I'd be honest, but not too honest. Some things were private, after all. I pictured snuggling up with Blue and telling her everything. One of the nicest things about my familiar was that she wasn't given to gossip.

However, even as I pictured my farmhouse and those I loved within its old walls, my discomfort grew.

Could Alex hear the thumping beat of my heart? I stole a quick glance at him. If he was aware of my mounting discomfort, he didn't show it. His forehead was creased with concentration, his gaze on the road.

I closed my eyes and silently pleaded with the spirits. *Please spare us from the evils of the past.* But deep down, I knew it was already too late. Something terrible had happened.

As we approached the long driveway at Barnham House, I knew my apprehension had been well placed. Two police cars were parked at odd angles in front of the entrance. Their blue lights blinked silently, garish strobes in this usually quiet country neighborhood.

Without a word, Alex pulled up along the road. I unbuckled my seatbelt and leapt out of the car as gracefully as I could in my new dress and sandals. Alex got out of his side of the car and our doors simultaneously slammed shut.

A flash of blue and yellow told me Norman was on the premises. "I just got here," he squawked. "Too late. Too late."

Two police cars had parked at the bottom of the long driveway. When we arrived in front of the house, I gasped. I hadn't known what to expect, but it hadn't been this.

In front of us was a scene of terrible destruction—worse, even, than the mess Dennis had orchestrated earlier.

The scene was lit up by the garden and house lights. The digger, which the operator had abandoned in the back garden earlier, had been driven into the front of Barnham House.

The machine had done considerable damage. An entire bay window lay in jagged shards on the front garden bed. Wooden beams were shredded and tossed about like discarded limbs. Bricks were heaped nearby where the vehicle had taken down the surrounding wall. The digger now lay half in and half out of the house.

I stared at the destruction, shaking my head. It was so disrespectful to the history and craftsmanship of the house. Who was responsible?

And then I remembered the story of the man who'd driven his own car into his house. A car he claimed had faulty brakes. A car he'd bought from Dennis Ratslaff.

Two uniformed officers were on the scene and between them was the man I suspected was culpable for all this awful damage: Ralph Dawson.

Swaying, with his head hung low, Ralph was perspiring profusely and sweat stains bloomed from the armpits of his now ripped dinner shirt.

Ralph had a gash on his forehead, which was slowly dripping into his eyes. He swiped clumsily at the wound, smearing the red across his face. "He had it coming to him!" Ralph slurred. He was clearly very, very drunk. Far worse than at the restaurant.

My mind flashed back to dinner earlier. Ralph's mortified companion had asked for the bill, and they'd left the restaurant. Two, maybe three hours had passed since then, and he'd already been drunk at that point.

Where had Ralph Dawson been all this time? Drowning his bitterness at the pub? Swigging from a bottle of vodka on the street? How much booze did one person have to drink to produce the strange logic which had convinced him to drive the digger into this precious house? Surely he knew that 'tit for tat' was a fool's game. He couldn't pay Dennis back for the sins of his past by committing the very same ones now.

Speaking of which, where *was* Dennis? Surely a crime like this would have him center stage and boiling over with rage?

One of the officers began to read Ralph Dawson his rights.

He was still shaking his head and waving his fists sloppily, murmuring that Dennis had it coming to him. "Show your face, you coward!" he shouted. "Fight like a man."

Alex touched my arm and gestured to the road at the other end of the drive. We weren't the only ones who'd stopped to see what was going on. The top of the drive was filling with people. The closest neighbors had left their houses and walked over to get a closer look at what was causing the commotion. I spotted Bernard Drake and Vera's grandson, Neil. Someone must have alerted Arthur Higgins-bottom to the commotion at the house, for I saw him jump out of a vehicle that pulled up beside Alex's Jaguar.

Behind him, I thought I saw Gillian's blue BMW slow as it passed the driveway leading to Barnham House, but the vehicle was too distant for me to be sure. If it was Gillian, what was she doing out this late? She'd left the restaurant ages ago.

Norman swooped down and landed on my shoulder. "This isn't the worst of it, Cookie," he said ominously. "Follow me."

While the officers were busy arresting Ralph, Alex and I followed the parrot to the back gardens.

As the two of us jogged to keep up with Norman, my terrible feeling of dread intensified. Much worse than what I'd experienced in Alex's car.

Since I'd been here earlier in the day, someone had erected a barrier around the crude hole excavated by the digger. There were posts and flagging tape around the uncovered grave. I wasn't certain whether the police or the university technicians were responsible, but it was clearly meant to keep people out. However, there was a gap where some of the tape had been torn away.

Surely, Dennis hadn't continued to desecrate a gravesite? Even he couldn't be that disrespectful, especially knowing the police and the university were aware of the find.

"It ain't pretty," Norman said, stretching a wing toward the jagged hole.

As though I were walking through heavy, freezing water, I moved forward. Alex took my hand and joined me. I was glad to have the warmth and comfort of his presence. We approached the edge of the hole, and somehow I knew that this time there would be more than just a creepy skeleton down there.

I leaned over the edge, my heart pounding so loudly that it was all I could hear. Alex made a sound, but all I could see was blackness. I didn't have werewolf super senses, so I got out my phone and hit the flashlight app. As I played the light over the bottom of the excavation, I had to swallow to keep down my dinner. Hard.

At the bottom lay Dennis. His eyes and mouth were both wide open, as though he'd received a horrible shock.

And it must have come as quite a shock when he was stabbed with his own weapon. For I could clearly see one of his collection of Aboriginal spears. It jutted out of his chest, while a pool of blood had soaked through his starched white shirt.

There was no question that Dennis Ratslaff had breathed his last.

And joined the skeleton he'd so recently disturbed.

I recalled Jessie Rae's moans about the spirits being disturbed, but no spirit had picked up a spear and stabbed Dennis Ratslaff to death.

His assailant had definitely been human and driven by rage.

CHAPTER 13

"What are you two up to?" A gruff voice demanded from behind us.

I turned to see a uniformed officer waving a flashlight in our direction. No doubt there'd been two teams of two and, sensibly, the pair not arresting Ralph Dawson were checking the premises.

I glanced back down at Dennis and gestured. I couldn't find the words. It was a terrible sight.

"You'd better have a look, Officer," Alex said calmly.

He came forward, a heavy-set young guy who couldn't be much older than Char. He searched both of our faces with his flashlight before turning it to illuminate the body in the hole. "Holy mother of God," he said, and I heard the lilt of an Irish accent.

"I know," I replied, shaking my head. "It's awful. I mean, Dennis Ratslaff was a menace, but this?" I glanced at his body again.

"You can't be here," the officer said, pulling himself

together. "This is a crime scene. Step back." He got on his radio while we retreated.

I was trying to process what had happened. The patio lights were on, and it was easy to see the empty space where one of the spears had recently been. There was no doubt where the murder weapon had come from.

After a short exchange on his radio, the officer said, "Go wait out front. Someone will be with you." He seemed both full of importance and nervous.

I bet this was his first murder. Poor kid.

As we rounded the house, Ralph Dawson was being maneuvered into the back of the closest police car. He was still protesting, though he showed no signs of sobering up. "Where are you taking me? I wanna go home."

The door slammed shut. Bernard Drake had explained to me why Ralph had it in for Dennis and his dangerous car scheme. Ralph had bought one of the dodgy cars and after a couple of months, the brakes went. The car broke through a fence and went right through a window into his front room. It was a terrible situation and could have ended in real tragedy. But destroyed roses, higher insurance premiums, and a replacement window surely weren't enough reasons to kill a man?

Or were they?

More police cars arrived, and then two detectives I'd met before turned up.

Detectives Michelle Rawlins and Dwight Evans had been pulled in now that this was a murder investigation.

Murder. The word struck my heart. Someone murdered Dennis Ratslaff.

In front of us, an officer was taking a statement from

Vera's grandson. Neil was standing a short distance from the other neighbors whose pale faces shone in the moonlight. Out of earshot so we couldn't hear what he said. Everyone was shaken up. Including me. Too much had happened in one day for this village. Collectively, we weren't used to this drama.

When Neil was finished, he came toward me. Neil's voice was clear, and I felt he was aware of his own importance at this moment. He said, "I heard the digger. Why would it be running at this time of night? I came to check and saw that man driving the digger," he said. "Anyone could tell he was drunk. The machine was swerving around the place."

"So you called the police?" I asked.

"Yes. But too late to prevent the damage to that beautiful old house." He sounded genuinely sad.

"What time was this?" He'd have told the police all this, but he didn't seem to mind repeating it.

"Around nine," Neil answered. "I know because I was trying to get the baby to sleep, so I was out, pushing her in the pram. It's the only way she goes down when she gets in a state. After I put the baby safely back inside my grandmother's house, I came here to see what was going on."

Neil seemed angrier than I'd expect from someone who was just visiting. Of course, Neil's temper had flared when Dennis had upset his grandmother, but why was he so caught up in this?

Then he partially answered my question by saying, "It's such a beautiful, historic property. There's no excuse for this kind of desecration."

Then, almost as though it had been whispered through the air, someone said, "What? Dennis Ratslaff is dead?"

I hadn't said anything and Alex certainly hadn't, so I wondered if someone had overheard the young Irish officer radioing in the death. Now that the detectives were here, it confirmed the rumor.

"Dennis Ratslaff had that coming," someone said. "It was pure payback for what he did to the people of this village."

"Karma," another person said.

I wasn't sure if they were referring to the destruction of his beautiful home or Dennis's death. If the latter, their comments were pretty bloodthirsty. I always thought of the residents of Willow Waters as peaceful people. Maybe I didn't know my neighbors as well as I thought I did.

Bernard Drake walked up to Sergeant Evans. "Excuse me," he said, "But I have evidence that may be pertinent. Earlier this evening, I was taking an evening stroll and heard raised voices. I heard *and saw* Ralph Dawson threaten Dennis Ratslaff." He looked around and seemed to realize he had an audience. He pulled back his shoulders. "Ralph Dawson came bowling up to the house. He'd obviously started drinking already. He said he couldn't believe that Dennis Ratslaff had the gall to show his face in Willow Waters again, let alone buy a property here. He kept screaming at him to leave." He cleared his throat and looked embarrassed. "I won't repeat the expletives exchanged by both sides."

He explained to Evans how Ralph Dawson had nursed his grudge from twenty years ago, when Dennis had sold him the car that crashed through his family home's front window. A few other neighbors chimed in, all validating Bernard's story.

Evans was taking rapid notes. "Please, everybody," he said, calm but desperately trying to keep up. "I need to speak with you one at a time."

I stepped back to give him space. I was happy to wait for my turn to give my statement. Besides, delaying would give me time to mull things over for a bit longer.

Something wasn't adding up.

I pulled Bernard aside. "I know we were talking about Dennis's sordid past just yesterday, but do you really think Ralph Dawson would commit murder over being sold an unreliable car?"

Bernard's eyes were full of sorrow. "I really want to say no, Peony. But all the evidence is pointing to yes. Ralph had the motive." Bernard shook his head sadly. He was a man who'd lived long enough to witness the frailty of human nature. "A long-held grudge can turn a warm heart to stone."

I glanced over to Alex, wondering if he was thinking what I was thinking.

His mouth was set in a severe line. "It makes sense," he said quietly. "I could see Dawson getting drunk and damaging property, but I wouldn't have thought he'd kill a man."

I nodded grimly. "My thoughts exactly."

Bernard touched my arm lightly. "This might not be the time to bring it up, but have you heard the latest about the bones found here?"

I admitted that I hadn't. In fact, I'd completely forgotten about what we'd uncovered only just that morning. It felt like a lifetime ago.

"Let me fill you in," he said quietly, though his eyes had taken on a sudden liveliness that was at odds with the somber mood.

And then Bernard told us that the bones had been handed over to the police earlier and given to the forensics department to assess their age. "Then a couple of the university's archaeologists drove over this afternoon to have an initial look at the site. They were understandably excited. Almost immediately, they unearthed a few pot shards and some coins. They're Roman."

"Really?" I was often amazed at how much ancient history was in this area. "You're saying that skeleton could be two thousand years old?"

He nodded. "We may have stumbled upon an ancient Roman burial site."

It might be, but Barnham House was now also the site of a recent death. A murder.

Had the killer been sending a message of some sort by killing Dennis in the graveyard he'd so recently desecrated?

I thought of the Roman tradition of throwing themselves on their swords. Had Dennis thrown himself on his own spear—with some help?

CHAPTER 14

For a village which was normally as placid as the sleepy river it was named for, Willow Waters was swept up in the intensity of all the drama at Barnham House.

Dennis Ratslaff's murder was all over the news. He'd been prominent enough that his murder made international headlines, especially as it was part of a larger story—the discovery of a Roman burial site. Archaeologists were only beginning their work, but they had already uncovered more bones and some tools that suggested the Romans had built their site atop an earlier Neolithic site.

I can tell what you're thinking—archaeology? Fast? But as soon as the bones were confirmed to be Roman, an archaeological team descended on the village.

Arthur Higginsbottom was beside himself with excitement.

As the head of the local historical society explained, to anyone who would listen, although thousands of years had passed since the bones had been buried, every site yielded new clues about how previous people had lived.

I met him Saturday afternoon lining up for coffee. Roberto's café was buzzing. Saturday afternoons were always busy, but the drama in and around the village had all of us chatting every place we met, which included the shops and on the high street.

I'm sorry to say that no one who knew Dennis seemed upset that he'd died. Those who did know him were unsurprised that someone had fostered a murderous intention—though they were taken aback by Ralph Dawson's arrest and mostly said he appeared to be a mild-mannered man, even if he was a little too fond of whiskey.

Many, like me, were aghast at Dennis's plans to rip up Barnham House's gardens and alter its interior as well. One thing was for sure: everyone had an opinion.

I wondered about Gillian Fairfax. I hadn't phoned or messaged her, after all. I wouldn't have known what to say. She'd have heard about Dennis's death by now. I wondered how she felt about it. After a short hesitation, she'd appeared thrilled that he was back in town, and practically the first thing he'd done had been to send her flowers. And then he'd asked her out for dinner. Dennis Ratslaff had not been a man to waste time. Including rushing to dig up the historic gardens.

The prevailing theory was that Ralph Dawson had killed his enemy in a fit of drunken rage. Since he'd been caught in the act of vandalizing the man's home, it was the logical conclusion.

However, I wasn't so certain. Would a drunken man really have murdered someone and *then* driven a digger into the front of his house? If you'll excuse the pun, it seemed like overkill.

I'll admit that my own head was swimming after last night, and I needed Roberto's strong espresso more than ever. The arguments at the restaurant, my kiss with Alex, Dennis's murder, giving a statement to the police: it was all too much. By the time I'd arrived home, Jessie Rae, Hilary, and Char had all heard about the murder from Norman. We'd speculated and theorized about the death and the discovery. The silver lining was that no one was as interested in my date as I'd imagined they would be. I was able to hold back the juicy parts of the evening, getting away with saying we'd had a nice time, and I hoped to see Alex again.

After I went to bed, I'd slept badly, dreaming of murder and foul deeds until even Blue got fed up with me tossing and turning and abandoned me.

Alex had dropped me off last night, given me a quick kiss, and said he'd call me. Okay, it was only a few hours later, but I wanted to talk everything over with him. I mean, even though the romantic end to our evening had been messed up, our first kiss had changed things for me. Before it happened, I'd not been able to imagine getting close to a man again. Ever. Now that I had, I felt...happy.

Did Alex feel the same?

"I took the liberty of suggesting that Dawn Fanning come and look at our site," Arthur was saying. He waited for a response, looking at me as if I should be impressed.

"I'm sorry, what? I mean who?" How long had the man been talking while I'd been miles away?

"Dr. Dawn Fanning," he repeated emphatically. "She's a renowned archaeologist with a well-regarded television show. You must have seen it, Peony. It's called *Digging into History*."

I could honestly say that I'd never watched anything with both digging and history in the title, and he seemed disappointed. I could tell I'd gone down in Arthur Higginsbottom's esteem.

He continued anyway. "I called her last night, and this morning she got on the road and checked into The Tudor Rose." His eyes sparkled.

Did the man have a crush? Or was he really just this much into history?

"Dr. Fanning is searching for a new project. She'll report on the dig as it takes place. It could be very exciting for Willow Waters if her production company chose us." He glanced at his watch. "She's now on her way for coffee with me. I've always longed to meet her. I cannot believe Willow Waters might be home to an ancient Roman site. Imagine."

I smiled. Arthur was glowing like...if not a kid in a candy store, then one in a museum's gift store with a hundred-dollar voucher. I wished my own feelings were that straightforward. Of course, it was exciting to discover what lay beneath the ground, but my mind was firmly on murder. As unpleasant as that was.

Char waved me forward, and I gave her my and Imogen's usual order.

"Are you doing okay?" she asked over the noise of the coffee bean grinder. "I mean, like, actually okay?" She'd dyed her hair last night, replacing the pink tips with purple. A thick swoop of plum-colored eyeliner matched it perfectly. Her large silver hoops jangled as she pressed the ground coffee into the portafilter (which I'd learned was the handle bit which held the coffee.)

"Mostly I'm just tired," I said.

"Norman's being clingy," she informed me, jutting her chin toward the door.

Sure enough, I could see Norman perched in the tree opposite Roberto's front door. He was staring at Char with an anxious look in his beady eyes.

"He was pretty traumatized. I'm glad you're letting him stay close."

"I made him promise he wouldn't do any more pooping target practice."

I didn't think he would, since his last victim had ended up dead.

After we left the murder scene, Norman had been quiet. And even this morning on the drive to Bewitching Blooms, he'd kept his comments to himself. I know, I could hardly believe it either.

I stepped to one side to wait for my takeaway, and Roberto took Arthur's order. I tried to block out the conversation around me, but it was impossible.

"Dennis Ratslaff got what he deserved," an older woman was saying to Vera, who was enjoying a pot of tea and some gossip. Milton was asleep at their feet.

"No one deserves to be murdered," she said, much kinder than her friend.

"After the way he treated you and Milton? You're more generous than I'd have been. And what was he thinking? Digging up that priceless garden?"

"I can't imagine."

"Your grandson saw Ralph Dawson do it, too. I wouldn't have thought of Ralph as a murderer, but you never know people, really."

Vera shook her head. "Neil didn't see Ralph hurt Dennis Ratslaff, dear. He saw Ralph driving the tractor, or whatever that digging machine is called. Ralph was acting erratic. That's why Neil called the police."

"They say Dennis was stabbed with an Aboriginal spear. I don't like to say he got what he deserved, but it's an odd thing to hang dangerous weapons in the garden. That's all I'm saying."

However, of course, the woman had much more to say, and Vera seemed happy to indulge her friend in a good gossip over tea.

Char's voice cut through the noise. "Peony? Your coffees." She handed me the two cups in a holder and a brown paper bag. "Thought you could use a couple of brownies, too," she said. "One for your energy and the other for Imogen having to put up with you."

I thanked her and was about to return to Bewitching Blooms when Arthur Higginsbottom waved me over. He was settling down opposite a woman who I took to be the famous esteemed archaeologist, Dr. Dawn Fanning. She had a broad, fresh face and smiled at me with a roguish grin as I approached their table.

Arthur introduced us, and Dawn stood to shake my hand. She was wearing wide-fitting jeans and a loose blue T-shirt, and there was something extremely youthful about her despite her whitish hair. As she shook my hand, I felt the woman's strength. Years of working outside on digs in all weather conditions had given her a solidity, and she moved in a way that was assured of her body's strength.

"Peony owns the local flower shop," Arthur explained.

"She was present when the bones were first uncovered," Arthur added. "You might want to talk to her—on camera."

"How fabulous," Dawn replied. "There's nothing quite so thrilling as the moment the soil parts and reveals its history. Why, I get shudders each time, and I've been doing this for decades. I'm excited to get to the site as soon as possible."

Arthur was so excited he all but jumped up and down in his seat. "I've told Dawn all about Lord Fitzlupin's brave leap into the pit. He saved that skeleton from obliteration."

"So did you, Arthur," Dawn said. "And I'm grateful. I have a bit of intuition about these things, and I think we're going to uncover something quite spectacular."

Maybe it was the comment about intuition, but I liked Dawn immediately. "Will you be starting work straight away?" I asked.

"No. I'm here to have a look around, talk to people, see if there's enough material to warrant bringing a camera crew and documenting the find. We also need the cooperation of the archaeological team." She paused for a second, her eyes shrewd. "But that's not usually a problem."

I bet it wasn't. So many people dreamed of being on TV, plus I bet it didn't hurt funding for popular projects.

"I'll be here for a couple of days researching." She paused. "I'll be dining alone tonight. Can I invite you both to join me?"

Arthur looked crestfallen when he said he had to decline as his grandson was having his birthday party, and his wife would kill him if he wasn't there. Dawn glanced at me.

I thought for a moment and then said, "The new vicar, Justine, is coming over to my farmhouse tonight for dinner. You're more than welcome to join us. I have two housemates.

One is studying classics." I pointed across the shop at the coffee counter. "Char is the other. And my mom will be there too. She's a medium, so I guess she's also interested in history, in a way."

I was pretty sure Dr. Dawn Fanning would turn down my offer of a family dinner that included a vicar, a student, a barista, and a medium, but she accepted with enthusiasm.

I wrote down my address on a napkin and said I'd look forward to it. "Come by at seven-thirty, and I'll introduce you to everyone properly. You'll soon feel at home."

I left the shop with my coffees and brownies, feeling a little brighter. Hilary would get a real thrill out of talking about local history with someone knowledgeable, and we might be useful, too, giving Dawn background information on the village and surrounding area.

On the way back to Bewitching Blooms, I spotted Sergeant Evans walking along the high street. I crossed the road and said hello.

He greeted me warmly, and I halted to ask how he was doing. Evans frowned for a moment before answering and in that split second, I saw the sensitive part of him which he tried hard to bury, and I knew that he was finding his job taxing. I couldn't blame him. There was no way he could have foreseen all that would land on his beat when he accepted a job in Willow Waters.

"I just met an archaeologist," I told him. "She works in TV, and she's thinking of using this find for a show, or series, I'm really not sure. It's exciting."

Evans smiled a little sadly. "I envy them, in a way. Dealing with deaths from thousands of years ago. At least you know the perpetrators aren't still out there."

Although he was wearing navy trousers and a smart white shirt, Evans looked a little rumpled. Clearly, he'd gotten about as much sleep as I had. Suddenly, I focused in horror on his right shoulder, where a blob of stuff sat that looked like Norman had used the detective for target practice. I didn't know whether to say anything, but the detective saw where my gaze had landed and made a face.

"I have a daughter. She's two this month. She likes to kiss me goodbye, and sometimes she's eating breakfast at the time." He brushed the gloop off his shoulder. "Porridge," he said, "I think."

"It must be nice having a little girl," I said, warming to him.

He let out a breath. "It's great. But sometimes I look at her and worry about what kind of world we're living in, you know? I want better for her."

"Well, by doing the job you do, you're making the world safer. Around here, anyway."

Evans's expression softened into a smile, and I saw my opportunity to dig a little deeper. "Has Ralph Dawson confessed to the murder?"

Evans squinted. "I can't discuss the case while it's ongoing, but...I can confirm that he's a person of interest."

Which I'd seen on the news, thanks very much. So, Ralph Dawson was admitting to operating the digger, but not to committing the murder.

I took a glug of my coffee and sighed with the specific pleasure of a caffeine fix. On impulse, I said, "When you have time, come into Bewitching Blooms, and I'll put together something for you to take home to your wife and daughter."

He shook his head. "We can't accept gifts because—"

"I'm not bribing you. Don't worry. I'll pull a couple of flowers out of my free bucket and wrap a bit of ribbon around them. Perfect for a two-year-old."

"All right, then." And he said goodbye and headed off.

I headed back to Bewitching Blooms with death on my mind. In the short time that Dennis Ratslaff had been back in the Cotswolds, he had upset a number of people. In fact, if there was an award for the most instantly obnoxious man, Dennis would win hands down. Though he might have some competition from Leon Barker.

If Ralph Dawson hadn't killed Dennis Ratslaff, there were plenty of other candidates. I ran through the list in my head.

Neil, Vera's grandson, had been pretty quick to blame Ralph. He'd called the police on the other man. But it would have been pretty easy, while Ralph Dawson was drunkenly crashing into Dennis's home, to grab the older man and kill him, then call the police and hand them Ralph.

But why would he? Had Neil enacted a terrible revenge on behalf of his grandmother? He clearly loved Vera, and I'd witnessed his rage after Dennis insulted and then almost ran over Milton. But murder?

Speaking of passion, although Gillian had been at dinner with Dennis the night he died, it was plausible the date was all a ruse. Dennis had betrayed her when they were young and in love. She might still be angry. I'd seen Gillian leave the restaurant and assumed that she went straight home, but what if she didn't? Could she have gone to Dennis's house? Perhaps she'd intended to smooth things over, but what if he'd been angry and dumped her a second time? Could she have erupted in a murderous rage? Did Gillian have it in her to stab her ex-lover in the heart?

And then there was Leon Barker, of course. His gym-fueled fury was pretty menacing, from what Alex and I had witnessed at dinner. I hadn't liked his jealousy and possessiveness. What had happened after he and Dennis had left the restaurant? Had they thrown a few punches and then slunk home? Or had Leon taken their argument right to Dennis's back door, with murderous consequences?

And then another terrible thought occurred to me. Arthur Higginsbottom. Now don't get me wrong, the man didn't exactly bring to mind a cold-blooded killer. Early fifties, a little portly, and a usually mild-mannered history nerd. Could he have wielded that spear to deadly effect?

For that matter, could Gillian have lifted the spear with her carefully manicured hands? I wasn't sure. But there's one thing I knew for certain: passion did strange things to people, including giving them superhuman strength.

"It's been busy while you've been gone," Imogen said, subtly reminding me that I'd taken an awfully long time to pick up a couple of coffees.

I handed her the bag of brownies Char had given me and explained about Dr. Fanning being in town. "She hosts a show called *Digging in the Dirt* or something."

"*Digging into History*," Imogen corrected. Unlike me, she knew all about the show and had even watched it. "It's pretty interesting," she said. "It's amazing how many historical sites there are all over the UK."

I settled in to work and noticed an enormous gap in the ready-made bouquet section of the shop. "Wait, you sold all of these while I was gone?"

"I told you I was busy while you were out."

"Okay, I'm back now. I won't leave again," I promised.

She watched me retrieve a couple of slightly imperfect Gerber daisies from the free bucket I kept outside the store. "What are you doing now?" she asked, sounding exasperated.

"I'm making a bouquet for a two-year-old," I informed her loftily.

CHAPTER 15

*S*ergeant Evans popped in and seemed delighted with the free bucket bouquet I'd made for his daughter. We sold out of all the ready-made bouquets, took a few orders for the following week, and I let Imogen go early and did the close-down.

By that time, Char and Norman were waiting at the Range Rover. As we were about to get in, Jessie Rae drifted up and climbed in, too. I'd imagined she'd drive herself to my place, but she'd obviously had other ideas. This meant Mom would stay the night, which she often did when she came for dinner. I sometimes wondered why she kept her own place, when she spent so much time at mine.

There was nothing I enjoyed more than arriving back at the farmhouse after a long day at work to the smell of Hilary's cooking. She'd been as thrilled as I'd hoped when I'd texted to tell her that Dawn Fanning was joining us for dinner that evening. With the addition of the archaeologist, that made six for dinner, which Hilary said was the perfect number for a dinner party anyway, and I was glad to finally make use of the huge dining-room table which could fit twice that number of dinner guests.

I wasn't so sure how the mix of dinner guests would get on, however. Char had a tendency to blurt out exactly what was on her mind. And Jessie Rae, well, she did love to speak with the spirits even when they weren't speaking back. I'd had a word with my mom about keeping her more eccentric traits under wraps, but you could never be sure with Jessie Rae. She was her own woman. Besides, she was still shaken up about the recent uncovering of those old bones.

It was going to be a lot for the vicar to handle, though I'd no doubt that Justine Johnson could handle herself. She was personable, good-humored, and had seemingly endless patience for the long stories many villagers liked to spin, which stood her in good stead for dealing with my mom. She also seemed like a woman who was open-minded, which you'd need to be to dine with two witches and a medium, even if you didn't know about the witches.

"Honey, we're ho-o-ome," Norman called out when we entered the farmhouse. He'd obviously rediscovered his mojo.

Hilary also called out to greet us.

Char disappeared to shower, and I followed the delicious scents to the kitchen where Hilary was slicing strawberries.

I told her everything smelled great and unpacked the bottles of wine I'd picked up from Vintners, the fancy wine store. I rarely went in there, intimidated by the staff who were all so knowledgeable about grapes and terrains, but after Alex's comments about his profession, I'd vowed to try to learn more and appreciate a finer wine. Don't groan at me, it's nice to take an interest in your friends' lives. The young sales assistant had been surprisingly friendly, and I'd left with four bottles that she'd insisted were crowd-pleasers without being too expensive.

"What's on the menu?" I asked Hilary.

After I'd texted her, she had insisted on catering for the dinner herself. Since the three of us had been sharing meals so often, we'd recently agreed to a house kitty where we each deposited some cash each week for groceries and house basics. It was a little like going back to my college days but with better housing. And I had my own room. And a garden and Blue too.

"I might have gone a little overboard," Hilary said, gesturing to the food.

"Have you been cooking for hours?" I asked. I knew how Hilary liked to follow recipes precisely, unlike Mom and me, but she was an excellent cook.

Hilary shrugged, clearly happy with herself, and told me that she'd prepped a sumptuous three-course meal. We'd be starting with a watercress and crème fraîche soup with herbs from the garden, followed by a slow-cooked chicken pie with corn crust and crisp green salad. We would finish with a strawberry pavlova.

I thought this sounded brilliant and told her so.

Mom drifted off to set the table in the dining room. I'd have to check later, as she had a tendency to forget what she was doing and leave the table half set, or put things like gravy boats out when there was no gravy on the menu.

"I admit, I wanted to impress Dr. Dawn Fanning," Hilary

said. "It's not every day we have a celebrity to dinner." Then, as though ashamed of her fangirling, she added, "And, of course, we're welcoming the new vicar. We want her to feel at home here."

"It should be an interesting evening," I said.

"What's Dr. Fanning like?" Hilary asked. "I have so many questions. Is she easy to talk to?"

"Very. I think you'll like her. I do." I grinned.

"I'm nervous that I'll talk too much or make a fool of myself," she admitted. "And I used to argue cases in court."

"You won't," I assured her.

Hilary surveyed her cooking. "I've made enough for a Roman army." She looked suddenly serious. "I'm not joking."

"Nothing wrong with leftovers," I said, and I helped Hilary clean up, load the dishwasher, and sweep the crumb-filled floor before heading for my room for a quick freshen-up. On my way, I peeked into the dining room, but Mom had done a perfectly good job of setting the table. Now she was outside talking to someone I couldn't see. Maybe Norman hidden in a tree. Or more likely a spirit.

There's not much point owning a flower shop if you can't provide a nice table centerpiece when you have a dinner party, and I placed the round arrangement of summer blooms I'd put together in the middle of the table. I loved the dining room with its rich polished floors, mullion windows, and antique pieces that Jeremy and I had picked up at auction.

"*Let peace, goodwill, and friendship fill this space,*" I whispered and then left to shower.

I found Blue asleep on the end of my bed. She woke up

when I stroked the soft tufts of fur on her belly—a sight I can never resist. She purred happily and rolled onto her back.

I showered quickly and then rooted around for a fresh pair of jeans that were devoid of pollen. I tucked in a black oversized cheesecloth shirt and finished the look with a gold necklace with a bumblebee pendant. I left my long hair to dry naturally. A swipe of lipstick and I was ready to be a consummate host.

Downstairs, I slipped into the dining room for a last look and to light the candles.

"Looks gorgeous," Char said, wandering in behind me and surveying the scene as well. "Nice to use this room," she added. Her hair was as wet as mine, and she wore an oversized black T-shirt dress.

Always looking for an excuse to get her working on her powers, I suggested that *she* light the candles.

She glanced around, looking guilty. Her powers were unwieldy and sometimes currents of electricity shot out of her fingertips. "But what if I burn down the house?" she asked in a low voice.

"You won't." I was training her to focus that energy enough to light candles. It was a useful and elegant way to practice.

She sniffed and scratched her head. "Don't blame me if I scorch the wood paneling," she said.

I felt slightly alarmed at the possibility but promised I wouldn't hold her responsible for a spell that I'd encouraged her to perform. "Just breathe and relax," I told her. "You can do this."

But she was too nervous. In the end, we took a candle

outside, and she got it on the third try, though the flame did shoot several inches up toward the sky before slipping back to normal candle-wick proportions. I blew out the flame and made her practice a couple more times until she was smoother, then we went back into the dining room.

She still appeared nervous, but I could see she had herself under control. She pointed at the other candle wicks and whispered, *light, bright*. The words didn't matter so much as focus and intent. I'd been doing it long enough that I could simply point to a candle and it would light. Soon she'd be doing that, too. For now, we were both pleased with her progress.

Even though I'd encouraged her to use her witch powers while we were alone, I reminded her that the new vicar was coming to dinner, along with an archaeologist who was also nonmagical.

"So, the new vicar?" Char said, narrowing her eyes so they all but disappeared. "Is she, like, very vicar-y? Remember, I literally escaped a convent before arriving in Willow Waters. I so don't want to be preached at all evening. It would be, like, my worst nightmare."

I assured her that Justine was very down-to-earth with a great sense of humor. I even went so far as to say that Char would like the vicar. She did not look convinced.

Just as Char was about to reply with something dripping with her usual sarcasm, Mom wandered in. She was dressed in an orange tunic with matching loose trousers. With her long red hair curling down her back, she looked very colorful. She was wearing a string of colored beads around her neck that rattled slightly as she walked.

"Ah, my sweet lassies," she said, looking at both of us with fondness.

Char couldn't have landed in a place where she'd receive so much unconditional love.

Hilary walked into the dining room and looked about approvingly as she unhooked her apron to reveal a charming twinset. And then the doorbell rang.

I opened the door. Justine and Dawn arrived together at seven-thirty on the dot. The vicar was holding two jars of homemade apricot jam, and the archaeologist held a box of truffles. I ushered them both in and introduced everyone.

"What a beautiful home you have, Peony," the vicar said.

Honestly, I never got tired of receiving compliments about the farmhouse. Although renovation was slow going (due to cash flow issues), small additions went a long way to making a house a home. For example, Char had fixed a swing bin under the kitchen sink which popped open when the door was ajar. She'd rewired my old six-slice toaster which had given up the ghost. She'd even rewired the dining-room chandelier which I'd bought at auction and then never got working myself. I was in awe of that girl's practical talents.

I promised a tour of the place but suggested a toast first. We went into the dining room, where both guests complimented me on the beautiful room. Hilary cracked open a bottle of perfectly chilled white Bordeaux (see, I told you I was learning), and the six of us settled around the candlelit table with a bowl of green olives to nibble on.

I poured each of the women a glass of wine and welcomed both the vicar and the archaeologist to Willow Waters.

We clinked, sipped, and then Hilary leapt up to tend to her starter.

So, as I've mentioned, I was a little worried about Char and Justine getting along, but that niggle was nipped in the bud when Justine swiftly brought up Char's truck.

"I saw you driving down the high street," Justine said, smiling at Char, "and I found it so inspirational. This might sound weird, but I've always wanted to drive a truck. Before I found my calling, I told my teachers at school that my ambition was to be a long-haul lorry driver."

Char almost spat out her wine. "You're kidding."

Justine shook her head. "Nope, not kidding. I thought it sounded so romantic. The open road. Me as the master of a massive vehicle. Just the radio and my thoughts."

"What about God?" Char asked, then looked as though she wished she'd bitten her tongue.

"And God, of course," Justine said. "He's always up for a road trip."

Char clinked glassed with Justine. "You aren't like the nuns."

"But the nuns are always with you, Char," Jessie Rae said. "They often surround you, and they're usually singing. It's lovely."

I knew my mother didn't deliberately freak people out, she just spoke as she saw things. Unfortunately, she saw a lot of things no one else did.

However, instead of looking at Mom as though she was crazy, Justine said, "You run the crystal shop, don't you?"

Mom looked delighted. "I do, indeed, lassie. I'm a medium from a long line of mediums. I'd be happy to give you a reading anytime. Though with that lovely pink aura you've got, I expect your spirit is in harmony."

Justine didn't remind my mother that they followed different belief systems, she just said, "That's nice to hear. I've always liked pink."

Hilary diverted the conversation when she'd returned from the kitchen and asked Dawn about the dig. "I was so intrigued when Peony told me about the site," she said breathlessly. "I hear there was a mosaic tile that could be from the Roman times, am I right?"

Dawn nodded and now her face matched the excitement on Hilary's. "The head archaeologist is an old friend of mine, so I was allowed full access. It's very exciting. Obviously, they've barely begun, but there were bits of mosaic tile, likely from a Roman villa, plus pot shards and Roman coins." She leaned forward. "However, and no one knows this yet, there are also animal bones and older coins. We aren't sure yet how far back the site goes."

"Wow," said Char. Even she was getting excited.

"I'm hoping to bring a film crew as soon as possible, get in on the ground floor, as it were. It's exciting watching the archaeology team making plans for how to excavate further. They usually work with two geophysicists to create a survey which maps the ground more thoroughly. Of course, the gardens are historic and so is the house, so we must work in a way that doesn't damage what's already there. Arthur Higginsbottom, the head of the local historical society, has been very helpful. I always find that working in harmony with all interested parties is the best way to proceed."

If only Dennis Ratslaff had shared her attitude, he might still be alive.

"The spirits have been very disturbed," Mom reminded us.

I was going to have to ask her to keep her spiritual communications to herself. We had a vicar and a scientist enjoying dinner. They might prefer to keep the spirits out of the conversation.

But, again, the vicar took Mom's comment seriously when she said, "People in the community have been disturbed, too. The death has sent shock waves through the congregation." She paused to look at Dawn. "But this can't be very interesting to you, as you don't know the community."

"On the contrary. While we obviously won't dwell on the murder during filming, if it hadn't happened—or if the victim hadn't begun digging up the historic garden—we'd never have discovered this historical find. I'll need to find a way of introducing the story that's respectful," she said, almost to herself.

"That won't be easy," Justine said, then grimaced. She'd briefly met Dennis, and he hadn't exactly made a good impression with his ranting and raving about pigeon poop, and terrorizing poor Vera and Milton.

"I guess this will be your first funeral in the village," I said, assuming that Justine would officiate at Dennis's funeral.

"I expect so, though no one has claimed Dennis's body," she said gently. "So currently there are no funeral plans."

What an awful thing to happen to a person—no matter who they were. We all fell quiet, except for Jessie Rae.

"A man with no family or friends," she said, shaking her head and then her beads. "How sad."

Hilary disappeared to the kitchen and then returned with

a huge Le Creuset pot filled with a delicious-smelling watercress soup. She had swirled the crème fraîche in a delicate
pattern on its surface, and everyone told her how lovely it
looked.

She ladled portions and passed round the bowls. There
was a pause in the conversation while we appreciated Hilary's
culinary talents. I was especially proud to know that the
herbs had come from our garden.

Char looked thoughtful. "What about Gillian?" she asked.
"Didn't you say that she was on a date with Dennis the night
he died? I've heard a lot of gossip at Roberto's, and they say
she knew him in Australia. She met him when she was
modeling there."

I nodded. Dennis had told me that himself.

Char said, presumably for Dawn's benefit as the rest of us
knew this, "Dennis was very wealthy and the village gossip is
that Gillian's on the hunt for her next rich husband."

"Village gossip can be very reliable," Dawn said. "I learn a
lot about communities in coffee shops."

"My gosh," Hilary said. "You're right, Char. Gillian was
probably the closest thing Dennis Ratslaff had to a friend—in
this village, at least—and she knew him in Australia. Perhaps
she knows who his next of kin would be."

"Things have not been going well for that woman," my
mom said.

"Is she a suspect in the murder?" Hilary asked.

I figured Gillian was keeping a low profile now that her
dinner date had been found dead, but I didn't think she was
being treated as a suspect. "It seems like the police are set on
Ralph Dawson as the killer. They found him at the scene,
drunk and belligerent. He was seen driving the digger into

Barnham House, and lots of people heard him threaten Dennis Ratslaff the night he died."

"Criminal damage is one thing," Hilary said, dunking a slice of baguette into her soup. "But murder? That takes a different kind of personality altogether. Ralph Dawson held a grudge, but even drunk, it's hard to imagine him stabbing someone."

I said I'd been thinking exactly the same thing.

"I'm not sure Gillian is mourning Dennis Ratslaff," Char said, "Today I saw her with another man."

I sat up straight. "A man with black, almost-shaved hair? And amber eyes?"

Char nodded. "Yeah. He was thickset and loud with it, too. I was taking a vape break from work out the back and saw him with Gillian. His silver Mercedes caught my eye, though it's a pretty standard model. Nothing to write home about. Gillian looked like she was trying to say sorry about something. She was leaning in, putting her hand on his arm, but he shook her off. His body language was like 'back off, babe.' You know what I mean?"

"That's Leon Barker," I said. "I first met him when I was delivering Gillian's flowers from Dennis. He also showed up at Gillian and Dennis's dinner in Kingham, and they argued over Gillian." I shivered at the memory. "It was ugly."

"Goodness gracious, what a complicated web," the archaeologist said.

"I promise it's not like this all the time," I said quickly, clearing the emptied soup bowls. I didn't want Dr. Dawn Fanning thinking Willow Waters was all intrigue and vendettas.

She looked philosophical. "I'm afraid communities have

played out these dramas for millennia," she reminded us. "As we uncover more bones and skeletons, there will be some tragic tales that will unfold. Jealousy, revenge, murder—these are not new."

Justine nodded. "That's true in my profession, too."

"And in the classics," Hilary agreed.

I turned back to Dawn, determined to steer the conversation away from the most recent murder. "When will you know more about what's buried in the Barnham House grounds?"

Dawn leaned in, clearly excited about the project. "It's only just begun. But I find the beginnings of a dig the most intriguing. You start out thinking you know what might turn up, but history has a way of surprising you. What we find will reveal so much about how lives were lived in this area many years ago."

"I just don't get how you can tell how old things are when they've been underground for so long," Char said.

"Well, it takes a lot of time and expertise. And in archaeology, you often find things from different eras buried in the same site."

"But don't you just find, like, shards of things? How do you ever know what it used to be?"

"I reckon you know more about that than you think, Char," the vicar said softly. She smiled at Char. "What with the way you fix broken vehicles and put engines back together again."

"That's right," Dawn said. "You take whatever's broken and then you put it back together, piece by piece." She lowered her voice. "I find the same thing is true with us humans."

Suddenly Jessie Rae began to sway in her seat, and her eyes fluttered shut.

"Oh no," I murmured, knowing a vision was about to rain down on Jessie Rae—and then us.

I opened my mouth to warn Dawn and Justine but then closed it again. I wouldn't be able to keep my mom's visions secret from the village's two newcomers for long.

"We see a priestess," Mom said. "So much finery. Incense and fire. Oh, the spirits are listening to you, Priestess. They are gathered round." She opened her eyes and gazed up into the air. "And they are hanging on every word."

Great. I invite the vicar round for the dinner, and my mom has a vision of her as a priestess. Now, I'd lived with my mom's antics all my life, but frankly, when she talked about spirits to strangers, it never got less embarrassing.

"Justine, I'm sorry," I said. "My mom, she has this intuition about—"

But Jessie Rae cut me off. "Why are you apologizing, lassie? It was a lovely sight. Besides, you're saying sorry to the wrong woman."

"I am?"

"Och, yes. It's Dawn, here," she said, turning to the archaeologist who was looking more than a little baffled. "Did you know you were a Druid priestess in your past life? Your ancestral line leads back to her. It's no wonder you chose the profession you did, dearie."

Dawn raised her brows. I was waiting for the customary nervous giggle which usually accompanied a newbie's reaction to my mom's visions, but instead Dawn just raised her glass of wine and said, "Well, I'll drink to that," and drained her glass.

The rest of us burst out laughing and followed suit, and then Hilary excused herself to check on the chicken pie.

I surreptitiously checked the vicar for signs of distress and was surprised to find her looking interested. My instinct about Justine hadn't been wrong. I was glad to have her at our table.

As Hilary portioned out the delicious-smelling pie, she said to Dawn, "Can you tell us any more about the dig? I would so like to know more about your procedures. And how you log what you find. If you don't mind talking about it, that is."

"I'm always happy to talk about archaeology. It's why I do the television program, really. I believe we need to understand where we've come from, who's gone before us, to fully appreciate who we are."

"Aye, the spirits agree with you, lassie."

Dawn took a bite of the chicken pie and let out a faint moan of pleasure. "This is sumptuous," she said. "The corn crusts. The tender meat. Wow."

Hilary beamed and said she'd be happy to cook for Dawn anytime. "Assuming you end up filming this find, and I hope you do."

"I think the chances are very good." She looked around the table with a mischievous grin. "In fact, I'm going to the excavation site later to pick up some papers. Would you like to come and see the set-up so far?"

Hilary clapped with delight, clearly thrilled, and everyone agreed that they'd love to see an excavation in progress.

"It's not that interesting yet," Dawn warned. "But you'll be among the first to see the fragments of mosaic and pottery and even a few bones."

"How thrilling," Hilary said.

Even though I'd been at the site and seen more than I'd wanted to, I still decided to tag along. Hilary's enthusiasm was catching. And how often would a renowned archaeologist be available to give us an after-hours tour of a dig?

CHAPTER 16

*I*f I say so myself, dinner at the farmhouse was a huge success. And after we gorged on pavlova, we all piled into two cars and drove to Barnham House.

I admit that I was a little nervous about returning to the scene of a murder. Nothing good had come from my visits to that grand house and its lovely gardens. First a boasting Dennis, eager to dig up and ruin his historic new purchase, then a skeleton in the garden, and then Dennis's dead body.

I reminded myself that Barnham House was simply a historic manor—albeit with a serious gash in both its front and back. I wondered what would happen to the house now that Dennis was gone. I hoped the new owner would treat the old girl with the respect she deserved.

Dawn and Hilary were getting on like best friends, exchanging their knowledge of the ancient Romans, which just so happened to be Hilary's favorite classical era. She was mostly a fan of the ancient tragedies and epics. Virgil's *Aeneid* was a subject she could hold forth on for as long as anyone would listen, and she loved the idea of combining her factual, ex-lawyer brain with the fictional land of her favorite author.

It was dark out, and for once I wasn't driving. I wound down the back window to let the cool night rush in. The village was quiet; the road was ours. I let the others chatter on and instead watched the landscape, listening for the faint hoot of owls. I was doing everything I could to block out the heavy feeling in my stomach. No, it wasn't that I'd eaten too much pavlova; it was that I couldn't help my thoughts returning to the sight of the dead man at the bottom of the hole he'd had dug.

After we reached our destination and exited the vehicles, Justine stopped as we passed the front of the house to remark on the destruction. "What a terrible thing to do to this beautiful old home," she said sadly.

Someone had boarded up the bashed-in front wall, and a sign warned people to keep back, as the structure was unstable.

Of the digger, there was no sign. Presumably it was impounded by the police and undergoing further investigation as part of the case.

Dawn led us to the site in the back garden. It was lit with a string of white bulbs, and a small white trailer had been driven onto the side of the plot.

"That's where anything we find will be examined and cleaned and then cataloged," she said.

I noted the electronic lock on the trailer. "It looks secure."

Dawn nodded. "Once we're properly up and running, we may post a night watchman, but that won't be my decision." She glanced around as though she might be overheard, but the only bird who could report what she said was currently at the farmhouse pouting because we'd told him to make himself scarce during our dinner party.

Dawn said, "The team has already found something." She paused. "I wasn't going to say, because we're not exactly sure what we're dealing with yet, but it's too exciting not to share. Want to see?"

"Oh yes," Hilary and the vicar breathed.

I glanced at Jessie Rae. She seemed pretty unfussed. I guessed that communing with the spirits meant she didn't think there was much special about digging up the past—she lived alongside it.

Dawn punched a code into the trailer's door.

I looked around and saw just how much work the team had already managed. It was amazing to me how long objects could lay undisturbed, keeping the stories of the human beings who owned them secret for years, even centuries.

Dawn opened the trailer door. She flicked on some lights, and then we filed in, one by one.

The trailer was nothing like I expected. It was full of expensive-looking computer screens and notebooks and some lab-style equipment I couldn't begin to guess the nature of. In the center was a large table, surrounded by Perspex boxes. This was clearly not a budget operation.

"I guess this is what the future of the past looks like," I said.

Dawn laughed.

"Woah, cool!" Char said, heading straight to a drone in one corner. "I have always wanted one of these. No idea what I'd do with one, but I want it."

Justine was drawn to the computers, and Hilary

approached the table. She bent over to peer closer at one of the Perspex boxes.

"You've got good instincts," Dawn said to Hilary. She opened a drawer and pulled out a pair of white gloves. "Want to see something truly ancient?"

Dawn opened the box and pulled out what looked to be most of a vase. "It's Roman," she said, "but in the most marvelous shape. Generally, we find shards of pottery, but every once in a while, we get a nearly perfect specimen. This is museum-quality."

Hilary gasped. Char was still busy admiring the drone.

"Of course it's Roman, lassie," my mom said. "I can see a centurion."

"Hush, Mom," I said quickly.

But again, Dawn just looked amused. "I have a feeling we could get rid of all this machinery and bring you on our digs instead," she said to my mom. "You could guide us."

"Och, well, you know I would like to diversify my talents, but the spirits don't work on command. They come and go. Like now. That handsome young centurion has gone. He was just a flash. You see, they only hang about if there's something they need to tell you."

Hilary peered at the vase. "Incredible," she whispered in reverence. "To think this has been buried in the earth for two thousand years. Here, in Willow Waters."

"What's this?" the vicar asked. She was pointing at some coins sheathed by a piece of thin plastic.

Dawn laughed. "That's a euro. Well, several euros, in fact, if anyone is heading to Spain on their holidays soon?" She grinned. "Lots of things are found on a dig that aren't of historical significance. We uncover all sorts. You wouldn't believe some of the things I've seen in people's backyards or stranded in the middle of a meadow."

"Och, do tell," my mom said, now fully engaged.

But I couldn't get into the moment. A sense of unease was spreading through my body, and I felt myself being called into the gardens. There was something, or someone, out there, in the dark. I could feel it.

I excused myself, saying I needed to get some air and left the trailer.

Outside, the feeling intensified. It was neither good nor bad. There was someone here. But why?

With mounting trepidation, I began to walk the perimeter of the garden. The string of white light bulbs cast shadows across the garden, while the lengths of the spidery plants reflected long spines on the side of the house. The tallest flowers swayed like drunks. Everything seemed calm, undisturbed. But I felt I was not alone. Visions of murder danced in my head. Ralph was not involved in those visions. Should I call out? But if the murderer had returned to the scene of the crime, perhaps I could catch him, or her.

Just as the thought flashed through my mind, there was a sudden crash, and I spun on my heels.

"What the—?" a man's voice said.

A familiar voice, but I couldn't quite place it.

"Who's there?" I called out, bracing myself and holding out my hands in case I needed to use my powers. But I didn't feel like I was in danger. More like I was experiencing an intrusion.

The silhouette of a tall, broad-shouldered man emerged from the shadows.

"Neil?" I said, shocked. What was Vera's grandson doing out stumbling around in the dark?

Neil came closer. He was red in the face, clearly as surprised to see me as I was to see him. "I'm looking for Milton," he said. "Have you seen him?"

"Milton, your grandmother's dog?"

"Yes," he said. He didn't seem shocked to find me here, and I didn't understand why.

"I was out walking Milton, and he wandered off. I thought he might have come into these gardens."

I narrowed my eyes. I'd never seen Milton go two feet from his owner, let alone make a break for it out in the dark alone. What was Neil really doing here? I recalled how eager he had been to tell the police about seeing Ralph raving drunk, threatening Dennis, and crashing the front wall in. Had he been too eager to cast suspicion on Ralph?

"Peony?" Char called out as she and my mom emerged from the trailer.

Neil's face turned an even deeper shade of raspberry. Obviously, he knew his presence in the garden of a recently-murdered man didn't look good.

Char stepped forward, putting herself between Neil and me. "Everything okay here?" she demanded in a menacing voice. That girl could have a third job as a club bouncer, as well as a second job as a car mechanic and general fix-it extraordinaire.

"Neil's lost his grandmother's dog," I replied lightly.

"You've *lost* a blind, deaf dog?" Jessie Rae repeated incredulously. "Och dearie, how on this earth did you manage that? It seems a little remiss of you."

"I told you, the little blighter wandered off," Neil

muttered, and then tried to turn the accusation around. "And what are you all doing here?"

"They're with me," Dawn said, stepping down from the trailer. "On official archaeological business. And you, sir, are trespassing."

The vicar joined Dawn's side, and Neil stared agog at the six of us. We must have made quite the sight. He mumbled something about really having to find Milton and left, calling the dog's name.

Had he forgotten Milton was deaf?

CHAPTER 17

I spent the following Sunday doing chores around the house. Under Norman's sarcastic eye, Char was tinkering with Frodo. Hilary was working on a school project, and my mother was off doing her own thing.

Hilary could barely talk about anything but the potential archaeological dig at Barnham House. While Dawn and Hilary were excited to uncover ancient history, I was more eager to understand the recent past. As I tidied, vacuumed, and dusted, I mulled over the death of Dennis Ratslaff and who, other than Ralph Dawson, might have committed the murder. Besides, deliberating about the weekend's events kept Alex off of my mind.

I hadn't realized I'd been waiting for his call until it didn't come. Two whole days of staring at the screen and I felt like a teenager after her first date. The guy I was crazy about hadn't called. But why? Why hadn't he called?

Looking back, it had been the perfect evening. Great conversation, delicious food, and wine. And then that beautiful kiss at the end of the night. The moonlight above us, the electricity between us. Everything felt right. And yet—no call. Not even a text. No surprise visit at the store. I hadn't even seen him at Roberto's. Was it possible that Alex had gone abroad on another work trip and not told me? Or was I stretching it too far?

I guess you're wondering why I didn't call Alex myself. I was a strong, independent woman, right? I didn't need to sit by the phone waiting on a man. But I guess something was holding me back, too. Was it shyness? It had been a long time since I dated, after all. I mean, more than six years.

Maybe it was because I wasn't sure whether I was ready to share my life with anyone again.

When I'd married Jeremy, I thought that was it. He was my person. My ride or die, as Char would say. I was never going to have a first date again, never wait for a call, never plan talking points ahead of time. I'd settled on the domestic life, and I'd been happy. I liked not having to ask for coffee because Jeremy had already made it for me before my craving kicked in. I liked always having a date for a wedding, a movie theater buddy, a warm and loving body there each morning, snoring gently. And when all that had been ripped away from me, I'd felt for a while as though my life had ended with Jeremy's.

However, I had the farmhouse; I had my mom; I had friends and a community and a business. I'd told myself that running Bewitching Blooms was enough. That Jessie Rae was enough of a family. That my friends and the coven were my life now. I didn't need a man. I didn't need to be in love.

I told myself that lie each morning when I woke and each night when I went to bed. But my feelings for Alex had sneaked their way into my life. I liked him as a friend, and I was attracted to him as a man. I'd even appreciated his loyalty and bravery as a wolf. Let's face it, I was a goner.

I was certain that he'd call Sunday evening. So certain, I checked my phone several times to make sure it was charged and the ringer was turned up.

He didn't call.

~

MONDAYS WERE ALWAYS BUSY. Our flower delivery arrived from the wholesaler and there were the online and phone orders to start preparing.

By the afternoon, Imogen and I were both ready for a pick-me-up, so she'd gone to Roberto's to pick up coffee and a treat.

I noticed Vera and Milton making their slow way to the greengrocer's. So, Milton had been found, then—if he'd even been missing. I watched Milton plod beside his owner and thought about stumbling on Neil in the dark at Barnham House on Saturday night. I hadn't bought his story then that he was looking for Milton. And watching the poor old dog, I was even more convinced that he hadn't gone missing. Something was off about Neil. In the brief moments we'd spent together, I sensed that he was covering something up. Whether that was murder, I wasn't sure.

As far as I knew, Ralph Dawson was still in custody. Did they have enough evidence to keep him there? I thought about the Aboriginal spear—the murder weapon easily accessible from the collection fixed on the outside of Dennis's house. It wouldn't be that easy to take one down, let alone undetected by Dennis. Unless you knew that he was out, of course, which was information that Dennis's neighbors would indeed have. Like Neil.

I wondered why Dennis had the spears in England, anyway. They seemed a strange choice of token to bring back from Australia. And as a murder weapon, it was also a strange choice. It would have been enormously difficult to maneuver, even if the person handling it was strong.

I thought again of Ralph Dawson, his thin arms and slight frame. It wasn't easy to imagine him, drunk, taking that weapon off a wall and then throwing it with such force and accuracy that he could kill a man with one try.

My reverie was interrupted by the sound of the store bell tinkling. Norman ruffled his feathers—his nap had been disturbed—and was clearly thinking about going back to sleep when he saw who'd entered the store.

I felt my own feathers ruffle.

"Gillian," I said, coming out from behind the counter. "How are you?"

I wasn't sure how else to greet the woman who'd so recently been on a date with a now dead man. I was conscious of how much tragedy had surrounded her these past few difficult months. First she'd lost her husband, now her old boyfriend.

She looked paler than usual, and her skin had lost its creamy quality. Although her blonde hair still shone like spun gold, it was in a less elaborate style, and she was wearing jeans and a white cotton shirt with no jewelry, no panache.

"Oh, Peony," she said, and to my surprise, she came closer. "It's all so dreadful."

From the lost look in her pale-blue eyes, she wasn't here for flowers.

"You must have had a difficult weekend," I said, recalling her standing there stunned as two men fought over her. Not that anything remotely like that had ever happened to me, but I felt it must have been awful for her.

She nodded solemnly. "It's been...a shock."

"For everyone, but especially you." I paused. Was it unfair to bring up Friday night's dinner at the trattoria? On the one hand, I didn't want to suggest that Gillian had been playing the field, but I couldn't very well pretend that I hadn't seen her at the restaurant. Or that she hadn't seen me and Alex, since we'd spoken to her.

The irony was that Alex had chosen the trattoria so we wouldn't be gossiped about by our neighbors, but Dennis and Gillian must have made the same decision. Even Ralph Dawson and his partner had turned up at the trattoria. I wondered whether he chose to dine farther afield, so no one would gossip about his drinking. Perhaps it was his dinner companion who'd chosen a restaurant a drive away from Willow Waters.

Then, even Leon Barker had shown up, though that was clearly no coincidence. For the first time, I wondered how he'd known to find Gillian there.

"I've had to speak to the police, of course, as I was one of the last people to see Dennis alive." Her voice wobbled slightly, but she could have been acting more broken up than she was. Gillian wasn't one for putting on grief. When her husband had been dying, she'd been so cool that I'd been shocked. Perhaps her feelings for Dennis went deeper than I'd realized.

I was happy to learn that the police were talking to more people than Ralph Dawson.

"But," Gillian continued, "everyone knows that Ralph Dawson killed him." She put a hand to her face, which muffled her words, "And with one of his own spears."

Had Gillian seen those spears with her own eyes? If so, she'd been at Barnham House, but that didn't make her a killer. Besides, everyone in Willow Waters with functioning ears knew how Dennis Ratslaff had been killed.

I took a look at her arms. They were covered by her shirt, but I'd seen her in tennis whites. She had a personal trainer and a tennis pro whom she worked out with regularly. I was fairly certain that she'd be strong enough to stab Dennis Ratslaff. The only question was, why would she?

"I shouldn't have gone to dinner with Dennis," she said, as though desperate to unload.

I didn't think Gillian had a lot of women friends to talk to. Frankly, I didn't think she had a lot of friends. Period.

"But I was flattered. He remembered me and seemed keen to rekindle our romance. And he was so rich." She shook her head. "But it was a mistake. I knew almost at once that Dennis wasn't going to give me what I wanted." She walked over to a bucket of roses and touched a velvet petal. "Leon won't speak to me now," she said.

"How did Leon find out that you were having dinner with Dennis?"

Her lost look was replaced by anger. "My maid. Now my ex-maid. Leon didn't believe me when I told him I was going to the pictures. It was a stupid excuse, now that I think of it. Anyway, he came to the house to check up on me. Perhaps he thought I had a man with me. He was always coming by at odd times, like the time you saw him. At first, I thought he missed me, but I now think he was checking that I wasn't seeing another man. So possessive."

I thought it was a good thing that they'd broken up, but I kept my mouth shut.

"Anyway, Leon asked where I was, and my maid told him I'd driven off to dinner in a red convertible with a man. Of course, everyone was talking about Dennis's Lamborghini. Leon must have driven to every restaurant within twenty miles, searching for us. Well, you know the rest."

"Not all of it. What happened with Dennis and Leon after he showed up at dinner?" Char had reported that the men had not indulged in the fistfight I'd seen brewing because a family with children was in sight. They'd driven off separately instead.

Gillian glanced around the store, even though it was empty. Well, except for Normie, but she neglected to look up. Norman was all ears, but had stayed unusually quiet. Was this him listening for clues, too?

"Honestly, I don't know what happened," she said. "You saw me leave."

I'd watched enough episodes of *CSI* to know that anytime someone started a sentence with the word 'honestly,' it was likely that they were lying. I kept my gaze neutral and told her to go on.

"I wanted to escape that awful mess as soon as I could and jumped in the taxi. From what I can gather, Dennis and Leon were arguing in the garden but soon left. I hope Dennis paid the bill," she said, almost as an afterthought. "I'll never be able to show my face in that restaurant again. I've never been so humiliated."

I tried not to laugh. Of course, Gillian hadn't attempted to actually pay the bill that night herself. Dennis had ordered a bottle of wine, which cost more than plenty of people made in a month. I was about to tell her that Alex had paid the bill, but decided to keep my peace. It wasn't my business to tell. Besides, I was more interested in Gillian's actions that evening than in Alex's.

"And you went straight home?"

Gillian nodded and then lowered her voice again so that she was barely whispering. "I locked all the doors and windows that night. Well, first I fired Estella, my maid. And then I told Owen Jones to keep watch in case anyone showed up."

"Gillian, why would you go out with someone so jealous?" I asked. It was a personal question, but I needed to know what was going through her head.

But Gillian merely shrugged. "I think I might be...a bit messed up. My romantic track record is...complicated. I don't know what I want."

That was the understatement of the year. But the bigger trouble was that the men she chose had a bad habit of ending up dead.

"Seeing Dennis again brought back a lot of memories. You know I used to be a model, right?"

I nodded.

"Well, in those days, I did very well for myself. It doesn't always happen that way for a model. Usually there are years of struggle. Of terrible castings, bad casting agents, knock-backs and setbacks, and the bills piling up. But I was used to that world. My mother started me as a child model when I was two years old, and I never knew anything different. I'd been in the hair and make-up chair since I was five. And the success continued into my teens and then, by the time I was in my early twenties, I was walking catwalks. I traveled and earned a good living. That's how I met Dennis, on a bikini shoot on Bondi Beach. He was the most confident man I'd ever met."

I'm not sure I'd have used the word confident for Dennis. Cocky, arrogant, and pushy definitely made the list.

She paused and tucked a lock of blonde hair behind her ear. "Gift of the gab—isn't that what they call it? Dennis swept me off my feet. Before it all fell apart." She seemed to be looking into the past and not enjoying the view. "He was married and lied about it."

I shouldn't have been surprised, but I was. "He went after you when he was married?"

"I found out, of course, and we had a blazing row, and I demanded that he leave his wife. He told me to grow up, that I knew how things were, and then dumped me. I was furious and heartbroken. So, to have him come back now and try to woo me, telling me he'd never forgotten me, and now he was a single man—I was flattered. Tempted. So we went to dinner."

"Right. I'm guessing that you chose the restaurant?"

"Of course. I wanted to be far from Willow Waters and Leon. Until I decided which of them I wanted." Her lips thinned. "It wasn't as though Dennis deserved to know that I had another man in my life."

"Right." I hoped I didn't sound sarcastic, but I sure felt it.

"He reminded me of the old days," she continued. "He made me feel young again. And there he was, very rich, saying that he'd never forgotten me. That he'd turned over a new leaf. Now I'll never know." She bowed her head. "Though he did eye every pretty woman who came into the restaurant."

Suddenly I saw Gillian as a small child in front of the camera, being told to perform for the adults, judged solely on her looks, growing up too quickly. I had a feeling that she defined herself by men. Never a good idea.

I said, "Maybe it's a good thing that Leon won't talk to you. He sounds jealous and possessive." I wanted Gillian to see that his possessiveness had the potential to be downright dangerous. I wondered if it already had been.

"Well, now there's no competition between Dennis and Leon, so Leon should be calmer," she replied, seemingly resigned to her fate.

That was not the answer I was hoping for.

"You know, it's only just occurred to me how little I know about Dennis, really," she said. "The police asked about his next of kin. They wanted to know about his relatives, but I couldn't help them. Dennis told me at dinner he and his ex-wife haven't spoken in years. He had no children. As far as I knew, he only had cousins, and I'd no idea where they lived."

"Did they ask you anything else?"

"I'd already given a statement. I was pretty worried about it, actually, as I thought they might be trying to paint me as some aggrieved and jealous ex-girlfriend."

I raised my eyebrows as if shocked, even though it had occurred to me that the police might view it that way. "Did they really?"

"It's difficult to tell. So many people saw me leave the restaurant, including you."

I nodded.

"Then I went home, and that's where I stayed."

My tone was skeptical when I said, "You stayed home all that night after you left the restaurant?"

"Yes," she replied with an edge.

"But I saw you that night." Okay, I wasn't positive I'd seen her, but certain enough to call her out in case she was bluffing. I held my gaze steady on hers. "I saw you drive past Barnham House in your blue BMW after Dennis was found dead."

"You didn't tell anyone, did you?" she asked in a panic, thus confirming that she had been in the area when her ex-boyfriend was murdered.

And she'd lied to the police about it.

"What were you doing there?" I was pleased that my bluff had gained one truth, but driving by a murder scene wasn't a crime. Had she done more than that?

"I was going to Dennis's to make sure that he was all right," she told me. "Leon is much fitter. He's in the gym every day. He boasts about how much weight he can bench press. Dennis is tough, but he'd be no match for Leon in a fistfight." She tucked the already tidy curl behind her ear once more. "I didn't want Dennis to get hurt."

The cynical part of me wondered if she'd been doing damage control.

"So you saw Dennis?"

"No!" she cried. "I was going to stop in when I saw the police cars and all the people. I kept driving and went straight home. I never saw Dennis again that night." Her eyes went wide, and I could see genuine sadness there. "I never saw him again."

Was this the truth? She'd lied about going to see Dennis. Was she also lying about sticking him through with a spear?

My shop wasn't large, and I felt a bit claustrophobic all of a sudden, standing so close to someone who could have committed a violent murder.

CHAPTER 18

*L*ater that evening, I was trying to relax in my living room by reading the newspaper. Not the news, which was anything but relaxing, but the books section. Blue was curled up on my lap, purring. I let one hand stroke her soft orange fur and the other turn the pages. But I wasn't really reading. My eyes were unable to focus, the inky text blurring. I didn't need to read plots of other stories. I needed answers to the drama I was currently embroiled in.

Char was in the outbuilding that we'd turned into her garage, working on a car belonging to one of her coffee store regulars. My mom was next to me reading a new title on crystals she'd purchased for her shop. Her familiar—Loki, a wily ferret—was wrapped around her neck like a fur stole. Hilary was opposite us, tucked up on her favorite armchair, laptop open, researching a recent Roman archaeological dig. I should have felt quite content. The reason for my distraction?

I could sense Alex.

He was outside, probably in his guise as a wolf. I knew that he was keeping an eye on us. But I wasn't sure why he needed to do it as another being. Couldn't he just, you know, knock on the door and come in for a visit?

"Did you know," Hilary said, "that it's incredibly rare to find a complete, undestroyed Roman mosaic floor? Many digs uncover partial parts of the floor or some intact pieces. But finding something complete is very special."

"I didn't," I murmured, not really paying much attention.

"Wouldn't it be wonderful if we found a floor?" she asked.

"Mmm," I replied.

Hilary continued reading, obviously not noticing my lack of attention. "*A Roman spear is called Pilum*," Hilary read, "*which was unique because once it was thrown, it bent—so you couldn't throw it back.*" She looked up. "Ingenious, isn't it? Those Romans were so ahead of their time. Imagine if we found one buried beneath where Dennis Ratslaff's Aboriginal spear was used. What a meeting of worlds."

Suddenly, my mom sat up straight. Then she got to her feet.

"It's happening again," Hilary murmured, rolling her eyes a little. She had a real soft spot for my mom, but Hilary wasn't convinced by Jessie Rae's powers. Even her less cryptic visions sent Hilary looking for scientific explanations. I couldn't blame Hilary; she was a woman who respected science and facts. Oh, no. Why did she have to read aloud about spears? Had that triggered Jessie Rae?

My mom started swaying, her cream crepe pants billowing, gold bangles jangling. Her eyes closed, and she let out a soft moan. She did like to announce herself.

"Mom?" I said quietly. "What do you see?"

"We see the dog. Oh, the poor, poor dog. He's hurt."

"The dog?" I swallowed.

The last time my mom had seen a vision of dogs, it was at Roberto's café with Alex when she'd seen a pack of dogs howling. Fortunately, she hadn't made the connection that Alex was part of the pack.

"What's wrong with the dog?"

"He's so brave, so loyal, but he's hurt," my mom repeated.

Hilary put down her laptop and stared at me. I shrugged. But I was worried. More than worried.

"Where's the dog, Mom?" I asked in a voice as calm as I could muster.

Jessie Rae's eyes flickered open. "The vision's gone, but I was in a garden. A Roman centurion was standing guard. And there was a dog. It was hurt."

"Roman centurion?" I asked her. "Are you sure? The last time you saw one of those was at Barnham House. Is that what you were seeing?"

Hilary stared at Jessie Rae. "At the archaeological site?"

But my mom didn't answer. She looked perplexed. I shared her sentiment. I had been so certain that Alex was outside, guarding the farmhouse. I'd felt him near me. So why did my mom see him at Dennis's house? And hurt?

Well, I wasn't about to hang around waiting to find out. "I'll be back," I said to Hilary and my mom. And before they could ask any difficult questions, I sped out of the room, grabbed my keys from the table in the hallway, and left.

I drove as quickly as I could, rising panic in my throat at the thought that Alex might be hurt.

My headlights lit up the road ahead, but there was no traffic. I reached Barnham House, turned into the drive, and parked. The outside lights of the house were on. Perhaps they lit up automatically at a certain hour as a safety precaution.

Even with no owner on the premises, they continued to function. The boarded-up part of the house remained untouched. I'd have thought there'd be tradespeople working to restore the beautiful home, but perhaps, without Dennis or an heir to give instructions, it would sit there. It seemed a shame to leave the house vulnerable to everything from weather to animals to burglars, but I couldn't worry about that now.

There was one other vehicle in the driveway and it wasn't Alex's. It was a Mercedes, silver, sleek, and expensive-looking. There was more than one silver Merc in Willow Waters, but I had a suspicion that this one belonged to Leon Barker. What was he doing here? And where was Alex?

I was so sick of people trespassing on these grounds, I was tempted to put a protection spell around the perimeter.

I went round to the back of the house. Already sections had been cordoned off by the archaeological team, fluorescent orange rope replacing the yellow police tape. I stood still and visually searched the vast grounds, looking for any sign of a wolf. In the dim light, I couldn't see any movement. There was no sign of Leon Barker, either.

I fought off panic and tried to get a hold of myself. "Peony Bellefleur," I whispered, "you are a witch of great power. Now focus and try to feel where Alex might be. You can sense him. Just trust yourself."

You probably think I sound crazy, but believe me— getting back in your body and reminding yourself of your strength is sometimes the only way to get through a bad moment.

I closed my eyes and focused.

But when I opened them again, it wasn't Alex that I saw.

I'd recognize that broad-shouldered stance anywhere.

"Mr. Barker?" I called out. "Is that you?"

Leon Barker was standing by the kitchen doors, his back to me. When he heard me say his name, he spun round in a flash. His heavy frame was clad in its usual all-black attire, which matched his dark, shaved head. His strong jawline jutted out in a way which showed me he was already on the defense.

"Oh," he said, in his high-pitched voice. Clearly, he wasn't expecting to see me. I seemed to make a habit of stumbling across men in these gardens.

"The flower girl, right?" he said, voice thick with mocking.

"Peony Bellefleur," I replied, walking toward him.

My senses were still on the alert for Alex. Why had I been pulled here? Had Leon and Alex had a fight? Was Alex lying hurt somewhere, either as wolf or man? Leon was certainly sweating. Had he used that brute strength against Alex? The thought was unbearable. But I couldn't afford to lose my cool if I wanted to know what Leon was hiding.

"What brings you to Barnham House?" I asked, as though we were both out on an evening stroll and had met by coincidence.

Leon shrugged with an assumption of ease that I could feel was forced. "I was thinking of buying the place, now that it's back on the market. Came to take a look around, you know. See the bits the estate agents want to hide from you."

"But it's not back on the market," I said. "It's the site of a murder investigation and an archaeological dig. In fact, I'd say it's about as far from getting sold as a house could possibly be." I was bluffing. I had no idea what the status was of Barnham House, but I was fairly certain that the gossip would have been all over the village if the house was for sale again.

Leon was not a likable man, and his very stance irked me. He stood a little like Henry VIII in the paintings where he gazed down on the world as though he ruled all of it. "In my world, money talks. Anything can be bought for the right price."

Even if Leon really believed his own hype, it was beyond inappropriate to be snooping around the house of a man whom he'd been fighting with the night he died. On the other hand, it was exactly the kind of thing I could imagine Dennis having done. They were oddly alike, those two.

And then it hit me. Both had made their fortunes elsewhere and now wanted to buy up a corner of England.

And then another truth hit me—so hard I nearly gasped. I steadied myself.

"So, I take it, if you're looking to buy a place like this, that the ship business in Estonia is doing well." I didn't pose it as a question. Instead, I let the statement hang in the air.

Leon looked taken aback by my words. Then he looked proud. I knew that playing to his ego was a good way of getting answers.

"I've done well, yes." He glanced around. "I could buy this place ten times over."

And whoop-de-doo to you. How many corners had he cut? How many people had he cheated to gain so much wealth? Somehow, I suspected quite a few. As you may have figured out, I didn't care for Leon Barker.

"I guess you need to spend a lot of time in Estonia. Looking after things, supervising?"

He squinted his amber eyes, which in the fading light

looked even more creepy than usual. "I have management in place, but I make it a rule to pay surprise visits. Keeps the staff on their toes and stops them from getting lazy."

"Estonia's in the EU, right?"

"Yes," he said, looking at me like I wasn't the brightest crayon in the box.

"I bet you have euros in your pocket all the time. Probably pull them out in the supermarket instead of a pound coin. I hate when that happens, don't you?"

I watched Leon's body language carefully. He visibly relaxed, the tension melting away from his shoulders. I was no longer a threat to him. He thought I was a bit weird, but harmless.

"Are you looking for money?" he asked with a sigh. "Is it a donation of some kind you want? You'll have to speak to my financial manager. I could give you his card."

I shook my head and forced out a cold smile. "No, Mr. Barker. It's not money I'm after. It's the truth."

"What?"

Now I changed my tone entirely, dropping all the pretense. "What have you done to Alex Stanford?"

Leon looked confused. His brow furrowed like he was trying to do complicated algebra.

"I think you need to take your meds." He made a motion to leave, but I stood in his way. His amber eyes glinted. But I wasn't afraid.

"I know you killed Dennis Ratslaff," I said, "and I swear, if you've hurt Alex, I will not rest until you are punished."

CHAPTER 19

O kay, the second the words left my mouth, I realized that hadn't been a smart move. My fear for Alex had made me act rashly.

Leon Barker—a muscle-bound gym fanatic—spun around and grabbed one of the Aboriginal spears still hanging from the wall.

And now he was pointing it at my chest. I mean, what had I thought a killer would do when threatened? And I'd accosted him right by the wall where a collection of deadly spears hung on display. Nice going, Peony.

Great. This was just what I needed when I was trying to find Alex. I slowed my breathing. It was going to take all of my strength to keep that blade from stabbing me. And right now, I wasn't sure I had that much strength in me.

"Aren't you the clever girl?" Leon taunted me. "Well done, flower lady. I'd give you a round of applause if it wasn't for the weapon in my hands. I've trained for years in hand-to-hand combat. It's a hobby of mine."

Like I needed to know that.

"Dennis Ratslaff didn't deserve to die," I said, trying to keep my voice even and calm. I didn't want Leon to think I was intimidated by his spear. If you asked me, both he and his victim had been overcompensating for something.

"Ratslaff tried to move in on my woman. No one steals from Leon Barker." A cruel smile twisted his face. "Ask my former manager at the shipbuilding company. If you can find him."

"This isn't going to impress Gillian," I said, although I didn't know where the courage had come from to taunt the man in retaliation.

"What do I care what you think? Gillian Fairfax is begging me to take her back. I'll let her grovel a little more. She must be punished, too, for betraying me. Then, when she's sufficiently penitent, I'll move her into this house. Get her away from the memories of her dead husband."

His jealousy was so huge, so poisonous that I bet he was even jealous of Alistair Fairfax. I said, "Alistair Fairfax was a hundred times the man you are."

"I don't need a crazy woman bad-mouthing me."

Okay. So, I had been stupid to provoke a killer. I was so worried about Alex, I wasn't thinking straight. But instead of letting my remorse overcome me, I channeled into my fear that this awful man had harmed Alex. I needed to get out of here quickly. And alive. That would help, too.

I kept my gaze fixed on Leon and let my anger rise up inside me and fuel the energy swirling in me. It began in the pit of my belly. A fire whose flames licked and curled and grew stronger. Did I have the power to avert a deadly spear? I was soon to find out.

Leon raised his spear and pulled his arm back. I knew it

was going to be a race to see if I could stop him with my magic before that deadly weapon pierced my skin.

I raised my hands. "Back," I called out, addressing the spear rather than Leon.

I could feel the charge fizz at my fingertips, but before I could launch the force of my wrath, Dennis Ratslaff's voice boomed out of the darkness, "Don't you bloody dare!"

I jumped, but Leon's reaction was way more dramatic. He turned his head, and the spear, toward the voice. "You're dead!" he yelled as though he might not have finished the job properly the first time and he was ready to kill Dennis Ratslaff again.

There was a sound like a cackle.

"What the—?" Leon said, still staring in the direction the voice and then the cackle had come from—which was from the site of the excavation dig. Leon ran toward the dark hole brandishing his spear. "Show yourself, fight like a man."

"*Fight like a man,*" Dennis's voice mocked.

But Dennis clearly wasn't in the hole, and with a growl of fury, Leon turned back to me.

I would never say a mean word about that parrot again. Norman had given me a reprieve and time to gather my strength.

As Leon turned his attention and a deadly weapon back on me, saying, "I'll deal with you, first," the words of a spell formed in my mind.

I took a breath. Norman might not be my familiar, but I felt his strength adding to mine. I said:

> "*Earth, wind, fire, and water,*
> *Hear these words of your daughter:*

Let my strength triple-fold
Gather my powers and turn them bold
To push this man far from me.
So I will, so mote it be."

As Leon raised the spear, ready to kill me, my hands shot out. I felt the power run through me and Leon went flying, his feet tripping across the ground. He lost his balance and then, spear still in hand, he dragged down the tape surrounding the partially excavated hole and disappeared from sight.

Silence.

My breath heaved in and out. I was on full alert, waiting for the killer to climb out of the excavation and come at me again. A minute ticked by. Then another. I didn't dare go and peek over the edge into the pit in case he was waiting for me to do exactly that, poised to thrust that spear into me.

There was a rustle of leaves and then Norman flew over the pit, drone-like. I was afraid Leon might go for the parrot —and only hoped that the target was small enough and moving quickly enough that he'd miss. But after dipping down low, Norman circled the excavation and flew toward me to land on my shoulder. He said, in the Brooklyn voice I'd come to know as his own. "Bad man's gone, Cookie."

I walked forward to the edge of the excavation, steeling myself. What did Norman mean, exactly?

At the bottom of the pit was Leon Barker, impaled on his own spear. His face was frozen in disbelief. The last emotion that the cold-blooded killer would ever feel.

It was a terrible sight, and I drew my gaze away. But Leon had done this to himself. My magic did not give way to ill intent—only protection. It was like something out of Hilary's Roman stories. The Fates had judged Leon harshly, and he'd died by his own weapon.

"You saved me," I said to Norman. "Mimicking Dennis Ratslaff was brilliant."

"Yeah, yeah," he said, like he saved lives every day.

"Have you seen Alex?"

"Nope."

But would he recognize Alex if he was in his wolf mode? "He's here. We've got to find him."

Leon Barker was beyond help, so without stopping to call 999, I motioned for Normie to follow me and we raced back to my Range Rover. My mom's vision was haunting me, and I needed to find Alex.

Back behind the wheel, I took a long, deep breath before starting the engine. I had let my worry about Alex overcome my sensibilities and taunted a murderer. Now I needed to focus and see if I could find Alex through my senses. It might sound corny, but if I trusted my intuition, then I knew it would lead me straight to him.

"Drive, Cookie, drive," Norman insisted.

I heard the rumble of the engine, but the small voice inside me said to stay where I was. I killed the engine. "No," I said quietly. "There's something here."

I got back out of the car and retraced my steps. Without Leon Barker in my face, I could sense something by the herb garden. It was a being in distress.

I picked up speed and ran toward the fragrant bed. The skies were turning inky, and the moon was rising. I could just make out a furry mound beside the basil.

I ran it to it and, to my horror, saw the outline of a dog

curled into itself. "Alex!" I cried. But as I approached, I saw that the creature wasn't big enough to be a wolf.

When I drew closer and delved into the undergrowth, I recognized Milton—Vera's old dog, who was both blind and deaf. When he let out a small whimper, I knew he wasn't dead. Thank goodness.

I released a sigh of relief. The poor dog had trapped himself. He'd fallen into what looked like some old fencing. His leg had gone through the rotted wood, and he couldn't free himself. I approached slowly, not wanting to startle the blind, deaf dog. I placed my hand under his nose so he could smell me. Milton's head rose enough for him to lick my palm. His tail even wagged a little.

"There we go, old boy," I cooed. "I'll get you out of there."

I only hoped he hadn't broken his leg or damaged himself too badly. Vera would be distraught.

I managed to pull Milton's hind leg free. He stood and took a couple of steps. He limped, but the leg was obviously not broken.

"I'm so glad you're okay," I said as he snuggled against my T-shirt. I held onto him for a long time. I was giving comfort but also receiving it. I'd caused a man's death. Sure, it had been self-defense, and Leon Barker had been threatening me with the very spear that had killed him, but still. I was shaken to the core.

Even as I hugged the old dog to me, I wondered about Alex. Where was he?

The flashing of blue lights cut through my temporary relief. Who had called the police? The darkness hanging over the open pit confirmed what I already knew. Leon Barker was dead. I'd wanted to make sure Alex was okay before getting caught up with the police and the lengthy statement I'd be required to make. Would they believe me? Or would I be taken to the station to 'help with their inquiries'?

I hefted Milton into my arms, not wanting him to walk until a vet had checked him out. He was heavier than I anticipated. I watched as a squad car pulled up to the house—and was both relieved, and nervous, to see the police arrive.

"It's okay," I whispered to Milton, even though I knew he couldn't hear me. "We haven't done anything wrong. But I admit this does not look good."

When Alex's dark-green Jaguar crunched onto the gravel, I felt an enormous wave of relief. Somehow, I knew it was going to be okay.

I stepped forward as two police officers emerged from the car.

I said, "There's been a terrible accident, and a man is dead."

The two officers shot each other a look. They were both young men, one blond, the other brunette, and barely in their twenties. Their uniforms were crumpled, as if they'd spent the day in their patrol car. Clearly, this was not what they were expecting to deal with on a lazy Monday evening.

Out of the corner of my eyes, I saw Alex approaching. He was fine.

"We had a call about a tall man trespassing," the dark-haired officer said.

"Yes, he's the one who had the accident. You're going to want to take a look at the excavation site round the back. A man named Leon Barker is in there. He impaled himself on his own murder weapon."

"Murder weapon?"

I nodded grimly. "He's also the man who killed Dennis Ratslaff."

Alex came closer. "Leon Barker's dead?"

I nodded and shivered. "He tried to kill me." I turned to the officers. "He admitted to killing Dennis Ratslaff. Actually, he boasted about it."

"You've got the wrong man in custody for Dennis Ratslaff's murder," Alex said. "You might want to call DI Rawlins and Sergeant Evans."

One officer made the call while the other kept an eye on us.

"I'm so glad you're safe," Alex whispered. Bending, he gently slipped Milton from my arms to his.

The dog seemed to recognize Alex instantly and gleefully licked his face, tail wagging. I hadn't got such a happy greeting, despite being the one who actually rescued him. Must be a canine thing.

Once more, there was police activity at Barnham House. And so, once more, neighbors arrived by car and foot, gathering to see what was going on. For the second time this week, there was a dead body in Barnham House's gardens. I had a sudden flash of empathy for Gillian. She'd been instrumental in causing a murder. It was going to make her life in Willow Waters even more difficult than she was already finding it.

I turned to Alex, who was stroking Milton. "How did you know I was here?"

He paused with a hand on Milton's head. I sensed his discomfort. "This might sound crazy, but I could smell you."

"Wait, what?" I resisted the urge to have a quick sniff under my pits.

"It's part of my..." he cleared his throat, "condition. When I'm close to someone, I can tune in to their natural scent. And that includes when you release a pheromone in your sweat, when you're afraid or in danger."

"You're kidding."

Alex shook his head. "I thought I wouldn't get here in time. I felt your danger, but was too far away to run here as a wolf. I had to bring the Jag. What happened with Leon?"

I was about to answer when I spotted Neil and his grandmother, Vera, approaching.

"Oh my darling," Vera cried when she saw Milton. "We've been worried sick."

Alex handed Milton over to Neil, and Vera kissed the top of Milton's head and fussed over him. "We'll get you to the nice vet," she promised him. "And you'll have such a special dinner when you get home."

Neil gave me a pointed look, and I felt a sudden rush of shame for thinking he was up to no good on Saturday night. As it turned out, Neil had been telling me the truth about Milton's evening wanders.

"My poor boy still remembers the former owner," Vera explained. "He used to feed Milton these turkey treats he loved. He totters over all the time, trying to find him. It's heartbreaking, really."

At that moment, DI Rawlins pulled up in her car, parked, and came to join us.

"Ms. Bellefleur," she said. "My squad has filled me in on tonight's events, but you'll need to make a formal statement." Rawlins looked tired—as well she might, what with the goings-on in this supposedly sleepy, slow-paced Cotswold village. Her usually shrewd brown eyes were rimmed red, and although she was dressed in her usual all-navy ensemble, like the two officers on the scene, she was a little rumpled.

The police took over, and I became one part of the investigation. I knew I'd be at the station for some time, but I wanted to see Alex before this long day ended. He agreed to meet me at my farmhouse and let the others know what had happened, though I suspected the jungle telegraph had taken care of that already.

Then I began to rehearse a statement that would contain the truth, while leaving out such things as a magical parrot and a witch's spell.

CHAPTER 20

"*P*eony Bellefleur," Jessie Rae intoned in her strictest mom-voice as I walked through the front door. "I've been worried sick. You just ran out of the house and disappeared for hours. I had the spirits barking in both ears. You got yourself involved in another murder and didn't think to take us with you? What were you thinking? And yet here you are, flouncing home like you're a teenager, looking like you've been dragged through a hedge backwards."

I held out my hands, protesting innocence. "Mom, this is my home, remember? I can come and go as I please." I could see how much I'd worried her, though, so I softened and gave her a hug. "I should have taken you all with me. I could have used the extra power and support."

Char and Hilary appeared in the front hallway to join us. Blue was just behind them, her tail pointing to the floor. I bent down to pick her up and assure her that I was okay. She sniffed my T-shirt suspiciously, no doubt picking up on Milton's scent.

"I was going to take Frodo and find you," Char said, "but Jessie Rae announced that you'd be coming home soon." She had grease smeared across her face, and her nails were as black as if she'd painted them that way.

I said to Char. "Norman was brilliant. He saved my life."

"Wait, I want the full story," Hilary said.

I insisted that everyone let me get indoors properly and take off my shoes before I would explain the evening's crazy events.

The three women parted before me, and Hilary headed to the kitchen to put on the kettle.

I kicked off my sneakers, or trainers as they'd say in the UK, and steeled myself to relive the evening's events for the third time.

Slumping onto the kitchen chair, I allowed Hilary to pour my tea and began to tell my little family about the evening's crazy events and Leon Barker and his terrible deeds. But first things first.

"Ralph Dawson was at Barnham House's gardens on the night of Dennis Ratslaff's murder," I said, "because he was definitely driving the digger, which crashed into the front of the house."

"Payback for what Ratslaff did to Dawson's family home decades ago," Hilary said. "So Dawson was guilty of criminal damage, but not murder." She might not practice as a lawyer anymore, but she still thought like one.

"How did you know it was Leon Barker who killed Dennis Ratslaff?" Char wanted to know.

"Do you remember the coin that Dawn showed us when we all went to the archaeology site?" I asked. "Among the old Roman coins was a fairly new euro coin."

The three women nodded in unison.

"Well, it was then that I started piecing things together. I didn't know it yet, but somewhere in my memories was my first, and suitably unpleasant, meeting with Leon Barker, when he boasted about his shipbuilding business in Estonia."

Jessie Rae looked baffled. "What has a euro got to do with anything?"

"They have the euro in Estonia," Hilary explained in her best lawyer voice.

"Right," Jessie Rae said, flipping her long red curls over one shoulder. "I'm a citizen of the world—this one and the next. I don't worry about details."

"Anyway, after I bumped into Neil snooping around the gardens that night, my suspicions were taken on a false path. It was such a surprise to see him at Barnham House that I immediately recalled how furious he was at Dennis for almost running over poor Milton. He was so protective of his grandmother that it crossed my mind that he might have killed Dennis out of loyalty—no matter how misplaced it might have been."

"Hmmm, I was slowly coming to the same conclusion," Hilary agreed.

"Come on," Char argued. "Kill a man over a dog?"

"Some people love their pets as they do the rest of their family," Jessie Rae said, shooting me a sly look. "*Especially* dogs."

"Wait," Char said, furrowing her brow and directing her next question at me. "If Neil wasn't the murderer, then why did your mom have a vision of dogs?"

I looked at Hilary. I'd have to berate my mom for her slightly misleading vision later. "Actually, it was about

Milton." I explained about his penchant for wandering over to Barnham House for treats and how I'd found him there injured this evening.

"Poor Gillian," my mom said suddenly.

"You feel sorry for her?" Char asked, incredulous. "Really?" Char didn't have much time for women like Gillian, those who prized looks and riches above all else.

"Well, one minute she has two love interests, then poof, they're both gone," my mom said, shrugging.

"And, if she hadn't become part of a deadly love triangle, her two lovers might still be alive," Hilary said.

"Poor Gillian," Mom said once more.

"Maybe this experience will encourage her to be a little more selective in the future," Hilary said. My housemate had long sworn off men in favor of her studies.

What a bunch we were. I certainly wasn't much better. I looked at the clock. Nine p.m. Was Alex going to come this evening?

"Get to the good part," Norman insisted.

Hilary gave the bird a bemused glance, but she seemed to be growing accustomed to Norman's exceptional powers of speech.

I apologized and continued my story. "Anyway, I rushed over to Barnham House because Jessie Rae's vision showed that, um, Milton was hurt."

"You sure care about that dog," Char said.

"Leon was there. Obviously, I asked what he was doing on the property, then it came to me. The euro in the pit where Dennis had died. Leon goes to Estonia all the time, so he must have had a euro in his pocket and it fell out when he killed Dennis. Stupidly, I confronted him about killing Dennis."

My mom almost choked on her tea. "You did *what*, lassie?"

"I told him that I knew he was a murderer and then the next thing, he grabbed another enormous spear and—"

"Like the one that killed Dennis Ratslaff?" Jessie Rae shrieked.

"Exactly. And just as I was about to..." I stopped myself, conscious of how I'd conceal my next move as witchcraft from Hilary.

"Get to the good part," Norman insisted, saving me from finishing my sentence.

I switched gears, giving Char's familiar his due. "Norman saved me. He imitated Dennis's voice just as Leon was about to throw the spear. It spooked the man so much that..." I faltered a bit but went with the same explanation I'd given the police. "He tripped and fell into the excavation. He impaled himself on the spear."

Hilary said, "Goodness. A tale of jealousy, revenge, murder, and men falling on swords. It's like a lesson in classics. Have we learned nothing in two thousand years?"

"Doesn't look like it," Char said.

"I owe you the finest treats I can find at the pet store," I said to Norman.

He leveled his beady eyes at me. "You owe me your *life*, Cookie."

"It's true." I stood and went to the cupboard where I hid Norman's favorite dried pineapple snacks.

He flew over and gobbled the lot from my hand.

The doorbell chimed and all the familiars reacted. Blue

stood on the couch, looking ready to pounce. Norman tilted his head from one side to the other. Even Loki, who was more pet than familiar, raised her head and stared toward the front door.

"It's all right. It's Alex," I said.

"Of course it is, lassie," my mom said.

"Don't worry," Hilary interjected before my mom could embarrass me further. "We'll all make ourselves scarce." She gave Jessie Rae a commanding look. "*All* of us."

I mouthed a silent 'thank you' to Hilary and went to answer the door.

It was wonderful to see Alex on my doorstep again.

"Come in, come in," I said, a little shyly. I wasn't sure whether to hug him or kiss his cheeks hello, so I breezed through the awkward moment by waving him inside.

He stepped inside and then pulled me into his arms. He felt so strong, I leaned on him a bit.

"Was it all right?" He asked into my hair.

"Yes. I think so. I gave a statement and answered some questions. I didn't get arrested, so I assume they believed me."

"And now you're home," he said, looking around.

Through his eyes, I saw the polished stone floors, the warm wallpaper, and carefully chosen prints hanging on the walls. They weren't originals, not like in Alex's castle, but each one meant something to me.

"Yes. I feel so much better now that's over."

I walked him past the closed living room door. I knew Hilary, Char, Jessie Rae, and probably Norman were in there.

I took him into the kitchen. At the sound of our footsteps, Blue lifted her head. I froze—was she going to sense Alex's canine self and rush over to nip his ankles? But no, she merely narrowed her eyes and went back to sleep.

"Ah, tea," he said, seeing the cups that we hadn't had time to clear up.

I put the kettle back on.

"It's been a long night," he said, checking his watch.

For the first time, I realized he wore a Patek Phillippe. I swallowed. What *was* I doing with this British aristocrat? Was I just making a fool of myself?

As I made more tea, I told him all the details he hadn't yet heard.

"Brought down by the euro," he said. "I think it was always about money with those men."

"Seems appropriate that their deaths helped unearth a valuable archaeological find," I said.

When we were sitting over our tea, Alex said, "I think I owe you an explanation for my behavior."

I thought so too, so I nodded. He reached over to take my hands in his. Holding Alex's gaze wasn't getting any easier. His gray-blue eyes twinkled, and my breathing quickened.

"I should have called you to tell you what an amazing night I had on Friday," he said. "It was one of the nicest evenings I can remember. Even more lovely than the dinner at mine."

"I thought so, too," I replied, not wanting to reveal that I'd been confused about the lack of call, as well.

"I needed a day or two to think," he continued.

My heart sank. Was Alex unsure of his feelings for me? I knew that on paper we didn't make sense. I was an American-born flower shop owner. He was a baron who could trace his ancestry back hundreds of years. But I thought we'd been on the same page. Those differences didn't matter.

He gripped my hands tighter. "I'm worried. For you. For your safety."

"My safety?"

And then Alex explained that he was worried about losing control of when and how he shifted form. "When someone I care about is threatened, my anger takes over and I begin to shift," he said. "I can't always bring myself back from the brink. And when I do shift, my animal instincts take over."

"I saw that at the trattoria," I reminded him.

"Yes. You put your hand on my arm and that was enough to control my reaction. It was extraordinary. Normally, only George can control me, and he does it by locking me in the dungeons on full moons. I run wild, scratching everything, howling. What if I accidentally hurt you? It's... Well, it's a lot to take on."

I understood. It was on the tip of my tongue to tell him that he didn't have to worry about hurting me. That if something did get out of hand, I could use my powers to protect myself. But then my mouth snapped closed again.

"Alex, do you trust me?" I asked.

He nodded. "Of course. You know my deepest secret."

"Then I need you to trust that I have a way to protect myself, that you don't need to worry about hurting me."

He cocked his head. Confused.

"I wish I could explain more," I said, meaning each word. "But for now, this will have to do."

His eyes were intent on mine, as though he could read

me. "There's something special about you, Peony Bellefleur," he said softly. "Whatever it is, I respect it."

I smiled. He was still holding both my hands.

"Alex, earlier you said you could smell my scent from afar. I've been wondering what...?" Then, I couldn't say more. "No. Never mind."

Alex grinned and then released my hands to cup my face in his large palms. "You want to know what you smell like?"

Oh, he was good.

"You smell like a Parisian flower market after a warm April shower," he murmured. "Freesia, the freshest rose, and, of course, peonies."

And then he kissed me.

CHAPTER 21

*T*wo weeks passed and Willow Waters returned to normal. If Willow Waters could ever be called normal.

Leon Barker was posthumously charged with Dennis Ratslaff's murder, and Ralph Dawson was given two years suspended sentence with two hundred hours of community service for the damage he'd inflicted on Barnham House. Most of his community service would be spent helping repair the destruction he'd caused. He didn't have the money to pay for the sensitive restoration, but, surprisingly, Gillian had offered to pay for the work. She obviously felt some responsibility for the two deaths that had occurred there and perhaps was trying to gain goodwill in a community that didn't exactly shower her with the stuff.

There was great excitement about the Roman site that had been partially uncovered and would give us information on Willow Waters' Roman history. Most of the village was talking about it, rather than the deaths of Dennis and Leon.

Gillian had decided to take an early summer holiday and

escaped the gossip by spending the next month in the Côte d'Azur. I couldn't blame her. Despite everything, Gillian still had my sympathy. I knew it wasn't easy being a widow, but unlike me, Gillian couldn't stand being alone. Not even for a week. Maybe some time away would give her perspective as well as a golden tan. We could only hope.

It was a Wednesday. Imogen had the day off, and I was tidying up the store when Arthur Higginsbottom came into Bewitching Blooms.

I'll be honest with you—I hadn't given the man much thought over the past few weeks. He could be a bit of a busybody, and I found that small doses of the man went a long way. So although the dig was beginning—and that made Arthur, as president of the historical society, quite important —I hadn't given him much thought. Not since I'd wondered whether he might have been angry enough with Dennis to murder him.

I was alone in the shop, though Norman was outside, watching the world go by from his privileged spot up high.

"Good morning, Peony," Arthur said pleasantly as he came toward the counter. His strands of gray hair were combed neatly to one side and his red cheeks were gleaming with good humor. "I haven't seen you since that sad business at Barnham House. Mr. Ratslaff made a poor choice in his new home, but I suppose it ended well for the community, since he inadvertently discovered Roman ruins."

"Do you know if they found any of Dennis's relatives?" I asked, hoping that I wasn't being too nosy. "It seems such a shame for that huge house to sit empty."

Arthur nodded and told me that one of Dennis's cousins had been found but wanted nothing to do with the house in the village. "It appears that Mr. Ratslaff managed to upset distant family members, as well as his old customers. When the cousin heard about the murders, he said the house must be cursed and, anyway, he couldn't afford the upkeep."

"Two dead bodies found there in one week isn't the first thing I'd put on the sales brochure."

Arthur gave me a wry grin. "Three, if you count our Caesar."

"Caesar?"

Arthur laughed again. "Our skeleton. We've taken to calling him Caesar."

Historical jokes weren't really my thing. "Of course. But what will happen to the house if the cousin doesn't want it?"

"He's asked if he can donate it to the village. He never expected to suddenly get rich. He'd rather the house was used in a way that's positive for the village, try to repair some of the damage that Mr. Ratslaff caused."

"Wow. Does the council want it?" The property was gorgeous, but it was going to be expensive for the council to keep it up, too.

"Yes. The council have agreed. They want someone to rent it while the dig is going on and will lease it for the foreseeable future. Vera's grandson, Neil, and his wife, have already put their application in and, between you and me, it's looking good."

I smiled. "Vera will be pleased! I'm so glad she'll have her family close by. And it's a lovely place for her grandchildren to grow up. There are so few babies in the village, it will be nice for everyone."

Arthur agreed and then bent to smell some of the new white roses I'd ordered this week.

"Lovely, aren't they?" I said. "Is there anything I can help you with?" I wondered if he'd like some flowers or one of the gift items we sold. As I said, it was a slow morning. I could use a sale.

Arthur said, "I only popped by because I heard you're to be one of the judges of Willow Waters' grand garden competition."

I stared at him blankly for a moment and then clapped a hand to my mouth. "Gosh, you know what—I'd forgotten I agreed to be a judge." So much had happened since Justine, our new vicar, had asked me to be a judge that it'd flown from my mind.

"I'm pleased to tell you that I've been asked to judge as well. I look forward to some healthy disagreements. We must agree in advance that whatever happens, we'll remain friends."

I nodded, giving him a weak smile. He was joking, right? A village garden competition wasn't like the Olympics.

He bid me a good morning and left, sadly for me, empty-handed.

But a slow morning left me with no excuses to ignore the pile of chores which had been building up. We'd had a new delivery of gift cards, and I'd only gotten partway through checking off the delivery note and remerchandising the card rack.

I'd been busy with the cards for about half an hour before the bell dinged again. Before I turned round, I knew it was Vera and Milton from the tap-tap of her walking cane. I smiled to myself as I remembered Vera giving Dennis's expensive car a great whack with her cane. She was still full of beans, no matter her age.

I greeted them both and then went straight to my dog treat tin and fed my old friend Milton a liver treat. He gobbled it happily, and I stroked his thinning fur.

"I've just had Mr. Higginsbottom in," I told Vera, "filling me in on the goings-on up at Barnham House. I'm delighted that it looks like your family will soon become your neighbors."

"Thank you, dear," she said. "We found out this morning that their application has already been approved, so it's official. I wanted to get them a moving in gift."

It was my moment. "How about a beautiful, scented candle? I have a gardenia that is a real crowd-pleaser and will make any house immediately feel like home."

"What a lovely idea," she said.

I guided Vera to the home-gift section and took the gold caps off my sample selection so that she could try each scent.

"You were right the first time," she said, after spending several minutes deliberating. "Gardenia, it is."

I took a box from the shelf and said I'd throw in a happy new home card for free. "Think of it as Bewitching Blooms' welcome to the neighborhood."

I knew that small things like a free card went a long way to making my customers feel special. And after the month we'd had in the village, some good cheer and friendliness was definitely a good thing. Especially as I'd briefly considered her grandson Neil as Dennis Ratslaff's killer.

As I wrapped the candle box in some gold tissues, I whispered a quick spell for happiness and prosperity.

Vera was hard of hearing, but she was also distracted by the white roses, just as Arthur had been.

"They're new," I said, tying a white velvet ribbon around the box.

"Quite special," she mused. "I grow my own white roses, but these are exquisite."

I thought Vera's garden was something to behold and told her so. "Are you entering the garden competition? I'm a judge this year!"

Vera's eyes widened. "Oh, Peony, what an honor. You must be thrilled."

I didn't want to say that I'd given it so little thought that I had forgotten, so instead I just smiled. "It's going to be a lot of fun, I'm sure."

To my surprise, Vera raised her eyebrows. "It might be more work than you think." With that cryptic comment, she thanked me again for the card and took her gift, gently tugging on Milton's lead so that he'd wake from his half sleep and follow her from the store.

As she left, I heard a man's voice greet them both and smiled to myself.

"Hello, stranger," I said, as Alex walked in.

He lifted a brown tray and handed me a black Americano and a chocolate croissant. This guy was gaining himself some serious brownie points. Literally.

In the past two weeks, we'd had two more dates. A Sunday drive through the countryside, ending with a cream tea in one of the cutest tea rooms I'd ever visited. And an evening at a wine bar in the nearby village. We'd agreed to take things slow, and I liked it that way. We were both a bit cagey, each reluctant to share too much lest it scare the other one off. But the more time we spent together, the easier it was getting to relax around him. I could hear my mom saying the phrase, rolling the words in her lovely accent. *Just let go, lassie.*

"And hello to you, too," he replied, leaning in to give me a kiss. "You look lovely."

I smiled. I was wearing an old pair of black jeans and a short-sleeved white linen shirt. In other words, nothing special, though I had made the effort to tong my hair into loose curls.

He asked about my morning, and I told him the news about Neil renting Barnham House, but I suspected he already knew.

"I'm glad for Vera," he said. "It's not good to be alone." He paused. "I think I learned that the hard way. I saw Dawn at Roberto's," he said. "She told me that Dennis Ratslaff's Aboriginal spears are of great cultural and historical significance and should be returned to Australia."

I nodded, my mouth full of croissant. "Good. He had no right bringing them over here in the first place."

"Dawn's going to see to it herself that they are returned."

"And now we can get back to a quiet life," I said.

Alex looked at me and lifted one dark brow. "I *also* saw Arthur Higginsbottom. Do I understand you've agreed to be one of the judges in the garden competition?"

"Yes. The vicar asked me. I thought it would be a nice thing to do for the village."

Alex put down his coffee and laughed. "Beware. People here take that competition seriously."

"How seriously?" I asked, wondering what I'd let myself in for.

"You'll find out," he promised, a disturbing twinkle in his eye.

He had to be teasing me. A little friendly competition among the local gardeners? What could possibly go wrong?

~

Thanks for reading *Highway to Hellebore*. I hope you'll consider leaving a review, it really helps. Keep reading for a sneak peek of the next mystery, *Luck of the Iris,* Village Flower Shop Book 4.

~

Luck of the Iris, Chapter 1

I THOUGHT that judging the prettiest garden competition in a quiet village in the Cotswolds in England was about as low pressure as a volunteer job could get. Boy, was I wrong.

I mean, when people say it's a contest to the death, they're usually talking about gladiators in a coliseum. At the very least, some serious wrestling action. But a gardening competition? Apart from deadheading, death's not the first thing which springs to mind.

But wait, I'm getting ahead of myself.

It was a particularly warm day in July. I know the villagers of Willow Waters (Willowers, as we called ourselves) were getting worried that it was too late in the season for a garden competition. As a proud flower shop owner, the truth was I shared their concerns. However, nature was the greatest leveler: if it was a problem for one gardener, it was a problem for the rest. If one rosebush was overblown, the same was true for its neighbors.

In any case, the committee of Justine Johnson, the village's new vicar, Arthur Higginsbottom, the president of our local historical society, Bernard Drake, the church organist, and me—the only person on the panel who actually had anything to do with flowers, had organized our first judges' meeting. Justine and I were both brand new to this kind of thing and, I think, shared the idea that it was going to be a fun, pleasant way to spend a few afternoons.

I mean, who wouldn't like to go and nose around your neighbors' gardens without feeling like a snoop?

We could stroll about to our heart's content, admire their patch of blooming sweet peas or their flowering herb garden or whatever it was that they were so proud of, and then we'd reconvene to pick a winner together. Simple, right?

But what I hadn't banked on was how the competition captured the imagination of the *whole* village—not just those participating. The annual competition was the brainchild of the town council, devised as a way to encourage the green thumbs to keep up the good work, and perhaps to inspire those who weren't putting quite so much effort into their gardens to pick up the spade as it were. Because tourism is a very important industry in the Cotswolds, and the beautiful honey-colored stone cottages, the charming villages, and quaint shops are even more inspiring when surrounded by splendid blooms.

Not that there were many derelict patches of garden in our verdant village and its surrounding areas. Willowers tended to be very houseproud—or cottage proud, as the case might be. There were those who'd been living here generation after generation and had inherited their lovely homes along with a strong sense of pride in their surroundings. With this group, it was like they didn't want to let down their forebears who'd gone to all the trouble of building their cottages stone by stone and planting the willows that gave our town its name.

And then there were the more recent transplants who wanted to fit in, a lot of them from London, or less frequently from overseas, like me—though I had the strange honor of being the only American in town.

There were also vacation rentals, and there were plenty of those. The savvy owners understood that their properties should look as postcard-pretty as possible so they could charge the big bucks to visitors who flocked to the Cotswolds seeking its quaint charm.

I guess all this is to say—everyone was invested in making Willow Waters the prettiest village in all of England. In my opinion, we succeeded.

However, as more than one social commentator has pointed out, behind every peaceful, beautiful English village is an opportunity for darkness to thrive. Open the chintz drapes and peek inside the living room, where a cozy fire crackles in the grate and a cat lies curled on the couch, and you may just discover a body lying on the floor. After almost three years in the village, I was starting to understand that Willow Waters was no different. We had our share of village joy, but with it came darkness, too. Death was no stranger to this corner of the Cotswolds.

Order your copy today! *Luck of the Iris* is Book 4 in the Village Flower Shop series.

A Note from Nancy

Dear Reader,

Thank you for reading *Highway to Hellebore*. I hope you'll consider leaving a review and please tell your friends who like flowers and paranormal cozy mysteries. Review on Amazon, Goodreads or BookBub.

If you enjoy knitting and paranormal cozy mysteries, you might also enjoy *The Vampire Knitting Club* - a story that NYT Bestselling Author Jenn McKinlay calls "a delightful paranormal cozy mystery perfectly set in a knitting shop in Oxford, England. With intrepid, late blooming amateur sleuth, Lucy Swift, and a cast of truly unforgettable characters, this mystery delivers all the goods."

Join my newsletter for a free prequel, *Tangles and Treasons*, the exciting tale of how the gorgeous Rafe Crosyer, from *The Vampire Knitting Club* series, was turned into a vampire.

I hope to see you in my private Facebook Group. It's a lot of fun. www.facebook.com/groups/NancyWarrenKnitwits

Until next time,
Happy Reading,

Nancy

ALSO BY NANCY WARREN

The best way to keep up with new releases, plus enjoy bonus content and prizes is to join Nancy's newsletter at NancyWarrenAuthor.com or join her in her private Facebook group Nancy Warren's Knitwits.

~

Village Flower Shop: Paranormal Cozy Mystery

In a picture-perfect Cotswold village, flowers, witches, and murder make quite the bouquet for flower shop owner Peony Bellefleur.

Peony Dreadful - Book 1

Karma Camellia - Book 2

Highway to Hellebore - Book 3

Luck of the Iris - Book 4

Vampire Knitting Club: Paranormal Cozy Mystery

Lucy Swift inherits an Oxford knitting shop and the late-night knitting club vampires who live downstairs.

Tangles and Treasons - a free prequel for Nancy's newsletter subscribers

The Vampire Knitting Club - Book 1

Stitches and Witches - Book 2

Crochet and Cauldrons - Book 3

Vampire Knitting Club: Cornwall: Paranormal Cozy Mystery

Boston-bred witch Jennifer Cunningham agrees to run a knitting and yarn shop in a fishing village in Cornwall, England—with characters from the Oxford-set *Vampire Knitting Club* series.

Vampire Book Club: Paranormal Women's Fiction Cozy Mystery

Seattle witch Quinn Callahan's midlife crisis is interrupted when she gets sent to Ballydehag, Ireland, to run an unusual bookshop.

Crossing the Lines - Prequel

The Vampire Book Club - Book 1

Chapter and Curse - Book 2

A Spelling Mistake - Book 3

A Poisonous Review - Book 4

Great Witches Baking Show: Paranormal Culinary Cozy Mystery

Poppy Wilkinson, an American with English roots, joins a reality show to win the crown of Britain's Best Baker—and to get inside Broomewode Hall to uncover the secrets of her past.

The Great Witches Baking Show - Book 1

Baker's Coven - Book 2

A Rolling Scone - Book 3

A Bundt Instrument - Book 4

Blood, Sweat and Tiers - Book 5

Crumbs and Misdemeanors - Book 6

A Cream of Passion - Book 7

Cakes and Pains - Book 8

Whisk and Reward - Book 9

Gingerdead House - A Holiday Whodunnit

The Great Witches Baking Show Boxed Set: Books 1-3

The Great Witches Baking Show Boxed Set: Books 4-6 (includes bonus novella)

The Great Witches Baking Show Boxed Set: Books 7-9

Toni Diamond Mysteries

Toni Diamond is a successful saleswoman for Lady Bianca Cosmetics in this series of humorous cozy mysteries.

Frosted Shadow - Book 1

Ultimate Concealer - Book 2

Midnight Shimmer - Book 3

A Diamond Choker For Christmas - A Holiday Whodunnit

Toni Diamond Mysteries Boxed Set: Books 1-4

The Almost Wives Club: Contemporary Romantic Comedy

An enchanted wedding dress is a matchmaker in this series of romantic comedies where five runaway brides find out who the best men really are.

The Almost Wives Club: Kate - Book 1

Secondhand Bride - Book 2

Bridesmaid for Hire - Book 3

The Wedding Flight - Book 4

If the Dress Fits - Book 5

The Almost Wives Club Boxed Set: Books 1-5

Take a Chance: Contemporary Romance

Meet the Chance family, a cobbled together family of eleven kids who are all grown up and finding their ways in life and love.

Chance Encounter - Prequel

Kiss a Girl in the Rain - Book 1

Iris in Bloom - Book 2

Blueprint for a Kiss - Book 3

Every Rose - Book 4

Love to Go - Book 5

The Sheriff's Sweet Surrender - Book 6

The Daisy Game - Book 7

Take a Chance Boxed Set: Prequel and Books 1-3

Abigail Dixon Mysteries: 1920s Cozy Historical Mystery

In 1920s Paris everything is très chic, except murder.

Death of a Flapper - Book 1

For a complete list of books, check out Nancy's website at
NancyWarrenAuthor.com

ABOUT THE AUTHOR

Nancy Warren is the USA Today Bestselling author of more than 100 novels. She's originally from Vancouver, Canada, though she tends to wander and has lived in England, Italy, and California at various times. While living in Oxford she dreamed up The Vampire Knitting Club. Favorite moments include being the answer to a crossword puzzle clue in Canada's National Post newspaper, being featured on the front page of the New York Times when her book *Speed Dating* launched Harlequin's NASCAR series, and being nominated three times for Romance Writers of America's RITA award. She has an MA in Creative Writing from Bath Spa University. She's an avid hiker, loves chocolate, and most of all, loves to hear from readers!

The best way to stay in touch is to sign up for Nancy's newsletter at NancyWarrenAuthor.com or www.facebook.com/groups/NancyWarrenKnitwits

To learn more about Nancy and her books
NancyWarrenAuthor.com

facebook.com/AuthorNancyWarren

twitter.com/nancywarren1

instagram.com/nancywarrenauthor

amazon.com/Nancy-Warren/e/B001H6NM5Q

goodreads.com/nancywarren

bookbub.com/authors/nancy-warren

Printed in Great Britain
by Amazon

51892962R00129